OUTLAW IN INDIA

Outlaw in India

Philip Roy

RONSDALE PRESS

OUTLAW IN INDIA
Copyright © 2012 Philip Roy

RONSDALE PRESS
3350 West 21st Avenue, Vancouver, B.C., Canada V6S 1G7
www.ronsdalepress.com

Typesetting: Julie Cochrane, in Minion 12 pt on 16
Cover Art & Design: Nancy de Brouwer, Massive Graphic Design
Map: Veronica Hatch
Submarine Sketch: Philip Roy & Julie Cochrane
Paper: Ancient Forest Friendly "Silva" (FSC)—100% post-consumer waste, totally chlorine-free and acid-free

Ronsdale Press wishes to thank the following for their support of its publishing program: the Canada Council for the Arts, the Government of Canada through the Canada Book Fund, the British Columbia Arts Council and the Province of British Columbia through the British Columbia Book Publishing Tax Credit program.

Library and Archives Canada Cataloguing in Publication

Roy, Philip, 1960–
    Outlaw in India / Philip Roy.

(Submarine outlaw series; vol. 5)
Issued also in electronic format.
ISBN 978-1-55380-177-1

    I. Title. II. Series: Roy, Philip, 1960– . Submarine outlaw series ; vol. 5

PS8635.O91144O97 2012   jC813'.6   C2012-902660-3

At Ronsdale Press we are committed to protecting the environment. To this end we are working with Canopy (formerly Markets Initiative) and printers to phase out our use of paper produced from ancient forests. This book is one step towards that goal.

Printed in Canada by Marquis Printing, Quebec

for Angela

ACKNOWLEDGEMENTS

The people who enable me to continue writing this series are a growing number. I would particularly like to thank the students I meet in schools, and their dedicated teachers and librarians. They put a smile on everything. I must also thank Ron and Veronica Hatch, and Deirdre and Julie, at Ronsdale; and Nancy De Brouwer for her beautiful covers.

Family and friends who continually give me so much generous support are my mother, Ellen; and Julia, Peter, Thomas and Lydia; my brother, Don; my buddy, Chris, and Natasha and sweet Chiara; lovely Diana, Maria and Sammy; Zaan and Nicholas; Hugh; Lauri; Dale and Jake (the intrepid). And a special thanks to darling Leila, and Fritzi.

The heat of the sun comes from me,
and I send and withhold the rain.
I am life immortal and death; I am
what is and I am what is not.

— THE BHAGAVAD GITA

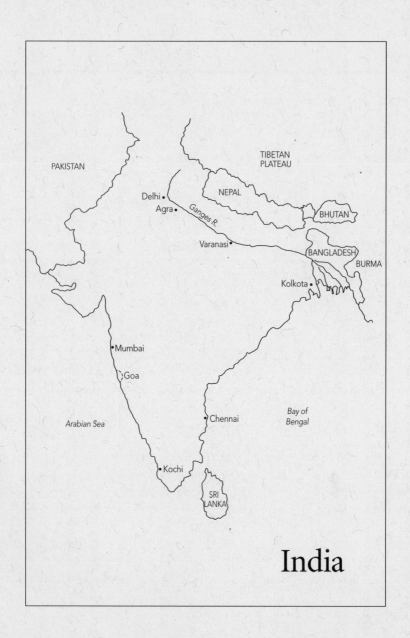

PAKISTAN

TIBETAN
PLATEAU

NEPAL

Delhi

Agra

Ganges R.

BHUTAN

Varanasi

BANGLADESH

BURMA

Kolkota

Mumbai

Goa

Arabian Sea

Chennai

Bay of
Bengal

Kochi

SRI
LANKA

India

Chapter One

I WENT TO INDIA TO EXPLORE. I wasn't looking for anything in particular, and I certainly wasn't looking for trouble, I just wanted to explore. Some of my discoveries were expected: the heat, ancient ruins, dangerous snakes and millions of people. But there were also surprises—both good and bad. And then there were a few things that seemed to find me, as if they had been just waiting for me to show up.

And of course I did.

We were sitting in the water off Kochi, in the Arabian Sea. It was late morning; the sun was high. I couldn't see it through the periscope but it was shining on the water. There were so

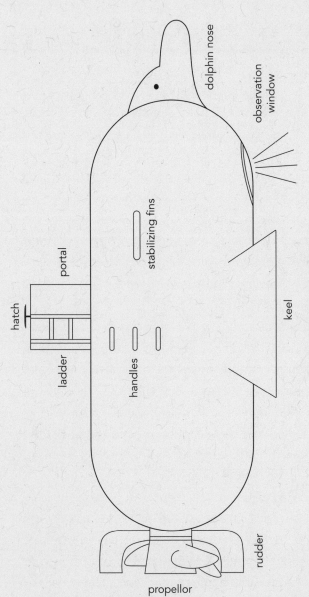

hatch

portal

ladder

handles

stabilizing fins

dolphin nose

observation window

keel

rudder

propellor

SUBMARINE SPECIFICATIONS

LENGTH: 20 ft. (25 ft. with nose and rudder) ❉ DIAMETER: 8 ft. (portal: 3 ft.)
MOTOR: diesel-electric (20 marine batteries) ❉ MAXIMUM SPEED: 21 knots by engine; 16 knots by battery;
5 knots by stationary bicycle ❉ MAXIMUM DEPTH: unknown ❉ RECOMMENDED DEPTH: 400 ft.
RANGE: 10,000 miles on surface; 20 hours submerged ❉ HULL: reinforced steel ❉ INTERIOR: wood

many vessels in the harbour it was hard to believe. My radar screen was crowded with blinking lights. We had just come from the Pacific where we could sail for days and days without seeing a single ship. Here it looked as though we had just stumbled into a bee's nest. There was a naval base here too, according to my guide book, but I couldn't see it. I wondered if the Indian navy had submarines.

We had been at sea for weeks now and were anxious to get out and stretch our legs and explore. If you stay cooped up too long you go crazy. But first we needed to hide the sub. Seaweed was already out, hanging around with other seagulls no doubt, and eating dead things. Hollie's nose was twitching, sniffing the smells of India that had seeped in when the hatch was open. He wanted out.

"Just a bit longer, Hollie. We have to find a place to hide first."

He looked at me and sighed. I steered into the harbour. Normally we would enter a harbour like this only at night, but with so many vessels who would notice the periscope of a small submarine? Who would be watching with sonar? It would be like trying to find a pear in a barrel of apples—no one.

I had never seen so many ships in one harbour before. It was incredible. There were freighters, tankers, barges, tugboats, Chinese junks, ferries, giant cruise ships, small cruise ships, sailboats, fishing trawlers, fishing boats, dories—everything but navy ships. Where were the navy ships?

The harbour was split into channels, like fingers of the sea,

Chapter Four

THE SUN WAS HOT ON my skin but not a burning heat. It felt like a heat you could get used to. The ground was warm, as if it were made for sitting on and lying down on and never feeling cold, at least not here in the extreme south of India, where it was always hot. Every country had its own feeling, it seemed to me. I liked the feeling of India already.

I think that Hollie liked it too. He seemed calmer, more relaxed and more reflective than before. There was something in the air here—the heat maybe, or the sun, or the smell of the land—that fired my imagination. Everything looked so different from everywhere else, and felt so different. And the feeling was pleasant.

and was a little confusing. The naval base must have been down one of those channels. Through the periscope I caught a glimpse of the Chinese fishing nets Kochi was famous for. They looked awesome. They were made of teak and bamboo poles and the nets hung over the water like giant spider webs. They were balanced so evenly it took only a few men to dip them into the sea and pull them out with fish. It was an ancient fishing method but was still used today because it worked so well.

I wanted to take pictures to show my grandfather, and then ask him why he didn't fish like that back in Newfoundland. My grandfather didn't like trying new things, which was why I liked showing him new things. I liked to challenge him. He'd make a face like a prune and say something like, "Don't fix it if it isn't broken." But I wished he could see these nets because I knew they would really interest him.

The oldest part of Kochi seemed a good place to hide. It was a seaport from the days of wooden sailing ships. There were ancient warehouses hanging over the water, and some were crooked and falling over. Broken piers stuck out of the water like reeds in a river. Some were broken in half like broken teeth. This part of the seaport had been abandoned a long time ago. Today all merchandise is carried in metal containers on giant ships that are loaded and unloaded by monstrous cranes in concrete terminals. When I turned the periscope around I could see the cranes miles across the harbour. Old Kochi was a ghost town now—a perfect place to hide a submarine.

I steered into a channel where the old warehouses were most rundown, and cruised along on battery power until I saw one where I thought maybe we could hide inside. The warehouse had a small boathouse at the very end of it, like a shack on the side of a cottage, and there was just enough clearance under water—about fifteen feet—for us to come inside. But I'd have to be extremely careful to not bump the poles or the boathouse would tumble down around us and maybe take the whole warehouse with it.

I was just about to steer in when I heard a beep on the radar. Another vessel was coming into the channel. I turned the periscope around and saw a small powered boat, possibly a coastguard vessel, coming in our direction. Shoot! I hesitated. Should we stay or should we go? Did they know we were here? Either it was a coincidence or they were investigating something they had picked up on radar but couldn't identify—us.

I shut off our radar so we would stop bouncing sound waves off them, which was one way they would find us for sure if they had sophisticated listening equipment, which they might have if they were the coastguard. I kept our sonar on. It was unlikely such a small boat would have sonar. I pulled the periscope down, let water into the tanks and submerged gently. We couldn't submerge much; the channel was only seventy-five feet deep. As we went down, I had to decide whether to sit still and let them pass over us, or take off. The problem with decisions like this is that there's little time to think; you have to choose quickly.

I put my hand on the battery switch and hesitated. The boat approached. Were they slowing down? If they slowed down we would definitely take off. No, they didn't slow down. So we stayed. They went over us and kept on going. Whew! Then, when they reached a bridge, about half a mile down the channel, they turned around and started back. Rats! That wasn't good. Now I had that uneasy feeling in the pit of my stomach that said, "Get the heck out of here!"

So I did. I cranked up the batteries all the way and motored to the end of the channel as fast as the sub would go on electric power, turned to port and headed out to sea. I watched the sonar screen to see if they would follow us. They did, although they didn't ride right above us, which told me that they knew we were here but couldn't locate us exactly. Maybe somebody had spotted us and reported us. That had happened many times before in Newfoundland.

We followed the ocean floor down to two hundred feet as we motored out to sea. It took awhile, and the coastguard boat followed us the whole way. Then I levelled off and turned to starboard. The coastguard kept going straight. Yes! We had lost them. They had never really known where we were; they had been just guessing. But we couldn't leave yet. We had to go back for Seaweed. I figured we could sneak in at night, when we'd look no different on radar from any sailboat. In the meantime, we could hide offshore by sailing directly beneath a slowly passing freighter, so as to appear as one vessel on sonar and radar. It was a great way to be invisible, though it was noisy underneath a ship's engines. We had done it before.

It didn't take long to find a freighter. I could tell what kind of ship it was even without seeing it, by its shape on the sonar screen. Tankers were easiest to identify because they were so big. Freighters had a sharper bow and flatter stern, as a rule, although the bigger the ship, the broader the bow. Sometimes older or smaller freighters had a pointed stern. This one was not very big and was only cutting twelve knots, which was pretty easy to follow on battery power. I figured we'd ride beneath her for ten miles or so, then find another freighter going in the opposite direction and follow her back. When it turned dark, we'd sneak into the harbour. Hollie took a deep breath and sighed.

"I'm sorry, Hollie. I'm trying. We really don't want to get caught."

We chased the small freighter for a few miles until we were right underneath her, then we came up to just twenty feet beneath her keel. Her engines were pretty loud. Suddenly she did something very strange. She turned sharply to port. That was odd. Why would she do that? Was she trying to avoid something in the water? Sonar didn't reveal anything in her path. And then, she turned *again*, to starboard. What was going on? Did she know we were here? I doubted it.

I was so curious I decided to drop behind, surface to periscope depth and take a peek. I dropped back a few hundred feet, came up, raised the periscope and looked through it. As my eyes adjusted to the light in the periscope, I got a terrible shock. The ship was battleship grey. She was carrying guns. She wasn't a freighter at all, she was a frigate, a navy frigate. We were tailing a naval ship!

Although I knew we were in big trouble I didn't quite grasp how bad it was until some sailors on the stern shot something out of a small tube-like cannon towards us. At first I thought it was just a flare—a warning—because it went through the air in an arc like a flare. But there was no coloured streak. Suddenly I realized what it was even before it hit the water. It was a depth charge.

"Hollie!"

I grabbed him, hit the dive switch and ran for my hanging cot. I threw myself on the bed with Hollie against my stomach just as the depth charge exploded. It blew up beneath us. It was like getting kicked by a horse. My teeth bit into my tongue. The blast hurt my ears, and there were strange sounds in the water following it. We were diving now. I held onto Hollie tightly and covered his ears. I wished I could have covered mine, because a second blast exploded right outside the hull. And even though my eyes were shut, I saw red. It blasted my ears so violently they started ringing and wouldn't stop. It was like being inside a thunder clap. The lights went out in the sub. The explosion knocked the power out completely. Everything went dark. And we were going down.

Chapter Two

A THIRD DEPTH CHARGE exploded above us. It rocked the sub violently but sounded to me like a door slamming behind a door that was already shut. My ears were injured. I kept Hollie's ears covered. A dog's hearing is so sensitive and I just couldn't let anything happen to him. I figured I would heal from pretty much anything. I didn't actually *know* that but I believed it.

There were no more explosions. I jumped out of bed, still holding Hollie against my stomach. I had to pull us out of our dive before we hit the bottom or reached four hundred feet—when pressure cartridges outside the hull would burst, releasing two nylon bags and filling them with enough air to pull us to the surface. It was the one safety feature I didn't want right now. I found my way through the dark to the control panel and flipped the emergency light switch. Soft blue light filled the sub. I glanced at the depth gauge: three hundred and five feet . . . three hundred and ten . . . I reached for the air switch and flipped it. Nothing happened! Oh, of course, there was no electricity. I rushed to the manual pump and spun the wheel with one hand while holding Hollie with the other. I listened for the sound of air but couldn't hear anything. I called out. "Hey!" Hollie looked up at me, but I couldn't hear my own voice. I rushed back to the depth gauge. Three hundred and fifteen feet . . . three hundred and seventeen feet . . . "Please stop!" . . . three hundred and eighteen . . . I felt the bow slightly lift. Three hundred and fifteen . . . Yes! We were rising.

At three hundred feet I opened the tanks manually and let enough water in to hold us steady. The sub stopped moving. At three hundred feet beneath the surface there was no current, light or sound. And we were dead in the water.

Since we had no electricity we had no sonar, and I couldn't tell where we were or even which direction we were pointing. We had about twenty-four hours of emergency light in the interior. We had at least forty-eight hours of air, probably more. What to do? If I could figure out what had happened to the batteries maybe I could fix them. First, I had to decide whether or not to surface.

The frigate wasn't trying to sink us; they were just trying to force us to surface. If they had wanted to sink us they could simply have fired a missile at us and we'd be dead now. It didn't surprise me they had attacked us. We were a foreign submarine following them in their own waters. It was the dumbest thing I had ever done. They didn't know who we were. They didn't know how big our sub was, or, especially, if we were carrying weapons. If I were on that ship, I would have done exactly the same thing, only I would have shot more than three depth charges.

But now what? I needed time to think it through. First, I figured I'd better check for leaks. I put Hollie down and went into the stern, picked up a flashlight, got down on my hands and knees and checked all the corners and edges of the floor of each of the compartments. Then I examined the walls and ceiling. There was no water coming in that I could feel. I checked the rest of the sub. The same. That was a relief.

Should we surface and give ourselves up? I looked around. The sub was our home. I looked at Hollie. He looked at me. I didn't know what to do, I really didn't. I didn't want to make things worse. What if they were just waiting for us to show ourselves again so that they could fire more charges? Or what if they had discussed it and decided that the next shot fired would be a missile? How could I know that they wouldn't do that? I couldn't. Therefore, I couldn't surface. The risk to Hollie and me was too great. What if the next depth charge blew a crack in the hull and we drowned before we had a chance to get out? No, as dangerous as it might be to try and run from them, it was too dangerous to surrender.

We had one thing going for us. I knew that they would be

listening very closely with sonar. I could imagine them standing around their sonar screen, with earphones on, waiting for the sound of our batteries spinning our propeller. As quiet as batteries were, they still created a faint whirring sound that any decent sonar system would pick up in calm conditions and clear water. And as they were sitting three hundred feet directly above us, they'd have no problem detecting us, and they knew it. They must have been assuming we were sitting still, which we were, or that we had sprung a leak and sunk, which we hadn't. In any case, they knew that the moment we started to move, they would hear us.

But that wasn't true because I had a stationary bicycle hooked up to the drive shaft, and the bike could turn the propeller without any sound at all. My mind drifted back to a day in Ziegfried's junkyard, almost five years ago, when we were standing around an old oil tank, which I had thought was a submarine, and he asked me if I could pedal a bike. I said I could.

Then he told me how a submarine had to have back-up systems to back-up systems for safety. Even then, the day after we had just met, he was already looking ahead to situations such as the one I was in right now. That's how cautious and concerned with my safety he was. And I had been so impatient so often over the two and a half years it took us to build the sub, because he insisted on taking extra time to prepare for the unexpected. Now that the unexpected had come, I was ready for it. Ziegfried—the greatest friend a person could ever have. How wise he was. How kind he was. How I missed him now.

I climbed up on the bike and started pedalling. It was very slow, just four or five knots at the most, but I could pedal all day if I wanted to because that's what I did everyday for exercise. Just an hour's pedalling would take us five or six miles away from the frigate and they wouldn't even know we were gone.

We weren't much further than five miles from land but I didn't know which way it was. We had been pointing north when we went down. Had the explosions turned us around? I couldn't tell. I knew that as we approached land, the sea floor would rise. If we went further out to sea, it would fall. Without sonar we'd only know the sea floor was rising if we ran into it. If we went slowly, at maybe two or three knots, hitting bottom wouldn't be so bad. Even striking a reef dead-on wouldn't be so bad. It wouldn't be any fun but it wouldn't be a catastrophe.

So that's what I decided to do. I pedalled gently and stopped every now and then to see if I could feel anything scraping against the keel. There was no point in trying to hear it because I couldn't hear anything. I had a constant ringing in my ears, which was very irritating. I tried to take my mind off it by concentrating on the pedalling. I also tried to imagine what we looked like from the outside, drifting silently through the dark water like a small whale towards the land.

Forty-five minutes later I felt a bump beneath my feet. I

stopped pedalling and let us drift. How I wished I could have turned on the floodlights outside to look down and see the bottom, if that's what it was. It must have been. I took the flashlight, went to the observation window in the floor of the bow and looked down but couldn't see anything. I climbed back on the bike and continued pedalling very slowly. Five minutes later we brushed against something again, and then we encountered resistance. I was guessing it was a sandy bottom. At least we were going in the right direction.

I pumped a little air into the tanks, rose fifty feet, jumped back on the bike and started pedalling again. Half an hour later we scraped the bottom again. I wanted to surface to periscope depth and take a peek but couldn't yet, just in case they had followed us. I was pretty sure they hadn't; otherwise they would have depth-charged us again. I wouldn't try surfacing until we were too close to land for them to blow us up.

Two hours later we were sitting on the bottom at one hundred feet. That was shallow enough. I pumped air into the tanks and we rose to just a few feet beneath the surface. I raised the periscope. I was dying to see where we were. It was hard to believe you were even moving anywhere when you had no means of checking your progress. It was very unnerving.

At first I saw nothing but darkness through the periscope. When I turned it a little I saw the lights of ships five to ten miles away. It was hard to tell exactly. I wondered if one of them was the frigate. I bet they had called other ships to join them. It was not every day they got to attack a submarine. Then I spun the periscope around one hundred and eighty degrees and got a fright. I was staring at a wall of lights. At first I thought they were the lights of a ship that was really close, and that they had caught us. But there were too many of them. It was a city. We were just offshore, maybe a quarter of a mile. I hoped it was Kochi. I didn't recognize it because I had never seen it at night.

There was so much sea traffic here we were going to get run over if we didn't get out of the way. None of the passing ships would detect us on radar because we were under water. But we couldn't surface and show ourselves either because the navy might spot us. What a mess! We needed a place to hide, fast, before the sun came up.

I had to keep pedalling until I found the harbour at Kochi. If I could find the harbour, I could return to that old ware-house and hide in the boathouse. Maybe it was crazy to go back there, to the very spot where we had been discovered. On the other hand, who would ever expect us to do that? Besides, they thought we were on the bottom of the sea.

Chapter Three

KOCHI HARBOUR WAS FILLED with lights, like Halloween, and people running around in the dark with flashlights. We came in without a light. I could have tied a flashlight to the hatch but it would have been too weak to resemble the light of a boat and might only have drawn more attention. I had to keep climbing the portal to look out and get my bearings; the periscope wasn't enough by itself for navigating in the dark. Without sonar a submarine is truly blind.

But I did manage to find our way, because I had to. There was no other choice. And the gamble did pay off. No one seemed to be looking for us. No one paid us any mind as we glided into the harbour as slowly as an old wooden sailboat dragging itself in on the power of a two-stroke motor. In fact,

I was pedalling as fast as I could and running up and down the ladder of the portal. I found the channel of old warehouses and steered into it. I must have climbed the ladder at least three dozen times by the time we coasted to a stop in front of the old warehouse. It looked pretty gloomy in the dark. And now the trickiest part: going inside the boathouse without the help of sonar.

The boardwalk of the boathouse, crooked as it was, sat about a foot above the tide. Even in the dark I could see where the barnacles lined the posts. There were two hanging doors that hung over the water, like barn doors, but had been shut and sealed a very long time ago. Boards had been nailed across them. I wondered when the last boat had come inside. Why did they keep a boathouse anyway? Was it for barges or smaller boats that went up rivers? None of the sailing ships could ever have come inside; their masts wouldn't fit.

I brought the sub around to face the front and submerged until the portal was showing only six inches above water. I didn't shut the hatch. Running up and down between the bicycle and portal, I pedalled us in under the hanging doors. Once we were inside the boathouse, I carried up a flashlight and had a look. It was like a barn inside, but a solid one that had only warped after hundreds of years of sun and wind and rain. On the far inside wall of the boathouse there was a door to the warehouse, but it was sealed too. I tied up the sub and carried Hollie out. Boy, was he excited! "We have to be careful, Hollie. This place is really old. Watch your step."

I couldn't hear my own words. Inside my head they sounded

like noises under water and far away. But Hollie heard me. He was a very cautious dog, especially when he sensed my caution. I stepped onto the boardwalk and put him down. It always felt strange to step onto ground that was not moving. It made you feel that *you* were still moving. Hollie must have felt it too.

There was a rusty old padlock on the door to the warehouse. I went into the sub and brought out a hacksaw and cut it off. Then I hung it back on to look normal. I pushed open the door. Dust burst from around the edges and I felt a brush of air on my face as we entered. I smiled. It smelled like spices and rope.

Hollie followed me in. I aimed the flashlight and saw an empty building with a balcony halfway up the walls and all the way around, and a stairway going up to it on both sides. The roof was supported by wooden arches, the kind you see in old sailing ships. That was cool. The men who built these warehouses were probably shipbuilders. I thought I felt something thump on the floor. But I couldn't hear anything. I swung the flashlight down and saw that Hollie had jumped. Had something fallen? I looked at the floor closely and saw Hollie sniffing at a rock. I pointed the flashlight up to the roof. Could it have fallen from there? That was weird.

We walked around and I was careful not to point the flashlight at the windows, although they were probably thick with dust. I didn't want anyone outside to know we were here. A second rock landed on the floor close by. I felt it, and Hollie jumped again. I spun the flashlight all around but didn't see anyone. That was strange; rocks don't come out of nowhere. We started up one of the staircases. I could feel the wood creaking beneath my feet but couldn't hear it. A third rock landed very close. I saw the dark shadow of it in the light of the flashlight.

Okay, I thought, somebody is here and throwing rocks at us. I picked up the rock, hurried up the stairs and ducked behind the balcony wall. Hollie hid under my legs and we waited. Sure enough, another rock came bouncing off the wall and landed beside us. I picked it up. Now I had two. I stuck my head above the wall just enough to see over it and swung the flashlight all the way around the balcony. Suddenly I saw an arm swing into the air and another rock come thumping beside us. Well, he didn't have very good aim, whoever he was, and he wasn't very big, judging by the size of the arm I saw. I felt like calling out, but what good would that do when I couldn't hear anyone call back? How long was my hearing going to be lost anyway?

Another rock came over the wall, and this time it ricocheted off the wall and hit my foot. Enough! I was afraid Hollie was going to get hit. So, I stood up, aimed the flashlight where I had seen the arm and I threw a rock there as hard as I could. I waited until I saw the arm swing again, ducked, and threw another one. Then I ran halfway around the balcony with my head down, aiming the flashlight, and threw another rock. It must have hit something or someone because I saw a figure start running away. I went in the other direction to cut him off, with a rock in my hand ready to throw.

We met in the corner. I shone the flashlight in his eyes and he squinted and stopped. He was just a boy. He made a dash for the stairs but I caught him, knocked him to the floor and held him down. He was as light as a feather. And he was so afraid. I shone the light in his face and saw his mouth moving but couldn't hear him. I could tell that he was really upset, but I wanted to know why he was throwing rocks at me. I held up my rock to show him. He winced and covered his face. "I'm not going to hit you," I said, but I couldn't tell how loud I was speaking. He looked at me strangely. "I can't hear," I said. I pointed to my ear and shook my head. "I can't hear. Do you speak English? Do you understand me?"

He nodded his head.

"If I let you up, will you stop throwing rocks at me?"

He nodded again, so I let him up. I held the flashlight so that we could see each other's face. "My name is Alfred. I'm a sailor. This is my dog. His name is Hollie."

He looked down at Hollie and his expression changed a lot. He bent down and started patting him. Hollie was a little suspicious but his tail started wagging. The boy patted him very gently.

"Why are you here?" I asked.

He looked up at me and shrugged.

"Are you hiding here?"

He didn't try to answer.

"Do you live here?"

He shrugged again and partly nodded his head.

"But . . . don't you have any family?"

He looked up and frowned, as if it were a strange question, and shook his head. I was guessing he was maybe ten years old; it was hard to tell in the dark. I didn't know what to do now. I didn't want him to see the sub. There were still a couple of hours before the sun rose so I figured I'd just sit down and wait. When the sun came up, Hollie and I would go outside for a walk.

I moved over to the wall at the top of the stairs and sat down. Hollie curled up beside me and the boy sat beside him and patted him. For a few hours we just sat there and I listened to the ringing in my ears. Maybe it was less now, I thought. I wasn't sure. Maybe I was just getting used to it. I wondered if there was a hospital here. There had to be a hospital in Kochi. Or maybe there was one in Ernakulum. That was the newer city across the harbour. The boy would know. When the sun came up and we went outside, I would ask him.

Finally, the sun squeezed in through dusty windows, with long golden fingers, and lit up the warehouse. It looked a lot friendlier in the morning. With wooden floor, walls and ceiling, and with iron strapping on the railings and balcony, it looked a bit like a giant sea trunk. The balcony made it look like a small theatre.

I was excited to get outside and see India. I would take money and find a bank to change it into rupees, and then find a hospital. But I wanted to get into the sub without the boy seeing me. I didn't know him or trust him yet, even though he seemed harmless enough. I turned towards him. He was just waking up. "Can you show me where you usually sleep?"

He pointed to my mouth and frowned. Then he dropped his eyes. He was extremely shy, or nervous, or both.

"Am I talking too loud?"

He nodded with his eyes opened wide.

"Oh. Okay. Is this better?"

He nodded again, got up and started around the balcony. Hollie and I followed him. On the other side he pulled a board away from the wall and pointed inside. I stuck my head in and aimed the flashlight. There were pieces of cardboard, a blanket and pillow, a few cans of food and some clothes. I saw a teddy bear. He looked too old to be sleeping with a teddy bear. "How long have you lived here?"

He put his finger to his mouth and frowned. Then he dropped his eyes again as if he were apologizing. He dropped his shoulders too. It reminded me of the way the smallest dog of a pack would cower to the bigger dogs, dropping its head and pulling its tail between its legs. He must have been afraid of me, I figured, though I had a sense that he was afraid of everyone. I tried to speak more softly.

"How long have you lived here?"

He shrugged. He didn't know?

"A year?"

He shook his head and raised three fingers.

"Three years?"

He nodded. I couldn't believe it. "Do you have any friends?"

His mouth curled into a smile. When he smiled, his eyes sparkled.

I convinced him to wait for me by saying I had to go pee. Hollie stayed with him as I went down the stairs and across the floor to where the door led to the boathouse. I closed it behind me, opened the hatch and climbed into the sub. I took my passport, two hundred dollars, and the tool bag for Hollie, for when he needed to be carried. I let just enough water into the tanks to lower the sub so that the top of the hatch would sit level with the surface, then climbed out and shut it. In the darkness of the boathouse you wouldn't even know there was a submarine there unless you went looking for one.

The boy smiled when I returned, and I asked if he would like to come outside with us. Nodding, he took my hand and led me downstairs. There was another set of stairs that led into a semi-basement. We entered a small tunnel that was probably a sewer. We had to crouch down. The tunnel went about thirty feet towards the channel. There was a grate sealing it, but the boy swung it open just enough for us to squeeze through. Then we climbed the bank and stood up in the brilliant early morning sunshine. I looked around in wonder. We were in India.

I had to find a bank and a hospital. And we had to find Seaweed. Well, actually, Seaweed would find us. There was no way in the world we could find him. All we had to do was stay out in the open until he spotted us. Seaweed could find a speck of rice on a sandy beach, and it wouldn't take him long.

I followed the boy down the road. We passed more empty warehouses and some houses. It was early but there were people outside already. Mothers were washing clothes and their children. The children stood naked while their mothers scrubbed them down with soap, then emptied buckets of water over their heads. Some kids were using the bathroom outside in front of everyone. That was weird. Then I noticed some people waking up on the ground. They had slept underneath blankets and newspaper. They stared at us as we passed. I tried not to stare back. But some people waved and I waved back. Hollie stared at everybody.

I asked the boy his name but couldn't figure out what he was saying, even when I tried to read his lips. I asked him if he knew where a bank was. He nodded. Was it open early? He shook his head. How about a hospital? He thought about it for a while, then nodded. I asked about a restaurant. His eyes lit up and he grabbed my hand and pulled me along. I freed my hand and followed him.

He led me to a corner in the road where a group of men were standing around a small portable food stand. I saw steam rising from a stainless steel container. The men looked old and tired but they smiled at us. They greeted the boy in a friendly way and wanted to shake my hand. One man slapped me on my shoulder in a warm and welcoming way. I pointed to my ear and shook my head. They looked sorry and nodded their heads. Then the man behind the stand took a ladle and scooped a hot brown liquid into two small cups. He offered them to us. I watched the boy take one with two hands, bring it to his mouth and sip it. He closed his eyes and smiled. So, I did the same. Then I smiled too because it was probably the best drink I had ever tasted. It was hot tea with lots of cinnamon, sugar, nutmeg and milk. It was so rich!

I asked the boy to tell them that I would return with money after we went to the bank. They shook their heads and said no, no money. The boy looked at me and shook his head too. I wondered if these were the friends he had smiled about. I thanked them and we followed the road to where the Chinese fishing nets were.

There was something hypnotic about watching the big nets swing down into the water and rise with fish in them. Half a dozen men worked each one while other men just stood around and watched. The nets never came up empty. I looked at the faces of the men who were watching. They must have seen this a thousand times yet they seemed fascinated still. I noticed there were no women here. I had seen women only at the washing. I tried to imagine my grandfather here. He wouldn't do it because he liked to work alone. He would respect it though, because it was a good method. It produced results. He just wouldn't want to do it himself.

When the bank opened, we were the first ones there. I put Hollie inside the mesh tool bag and hung it over my shoulder. He liked it and was used to being carried in it. It had a wooden frame and was just big enough for him to ride inside comfortably. He could see out but no one could see in unless they stood next to him and stared closely.

But the boy was nervous and didn't want to come inside the bank. I insisted because I needed his help. I couldn't hear. So he followed me in but a man stepped in our way, smiled at me but frowned angrily at the boy and pointed to the door. He barked something at him; I saw his mouth. I held the boy's hand but the man looked at me and shook his head. He ushered the boy outside, without actually touching him. I thought that was strange. I wondered if it was because the boy's feet were bare. "I'll be right out," I said to him, and I probably said it too loudly.

I changed my money from dollars to rupees and walked out with a fat handful of funny-looking money. Some of the bills were large and some small. I stuffed them into my pocket, let Hollie out of the tool bag and asked the boy to show me where the hospital was. He pointed up the road so I turned and started that way, but he lagged behind. When I turned around to see why, he came running up to me with something in his hand. I looked. It was one of the large bills. I counted the rest of the money and realized that I had dropped it, and he had found it. We stared at each other for a moment. He could have just kept it and I would never have known.

"Thank you," I said. He smiled and his eyes sparkled. I remembered once finding a twenty-dollar bill when I was little and giving it to my neighbour who had lost it, and she gave me a dollar as a reward. So, I took one of the smaller bills and gave it to the boy. "Thank you for your honesty," I said. He took it in his hands and stared at it as if he had never seen money before. And as we continued up the road, he never took his eyes away from it.

The hospital was just a small clinic. But they wouldn't let the boy in. He stood at the door with a deeply guilty look on his face, as if he had done something wrong. This time I asked why he wasn't allowed inside. A lady in a white uniform tried to explain it to me by writing a word down on a piece of paper. She wrote, "Dalit." "What does it mean?" I asked. She looked at me and frowned. She wrote another word underneath the first one. "Untouchable." Oh. That meant he was in the lowest class of India, or even lower than the lowest class. I wondered how she knew that. Could she tell just by looking at him? Was it because he was barefoot? Because his clothes were shabby? Was it the guilty look on his face? That went away when it was just him and me and Hollie.

So I asked the boy to wait for me again. He agreed. He pulled the bill out of his pocket and turned around to examine it again. I followed the lady to an examination room where she had me fill out a form asking for my name, age, address, passport number and what was wrong with me. I was waiting for her to tell me to take Hollie out too once she realized

I was carrying a dog on my back, but she didn't. She clicked her tongue and smiled at him through the mesh.

When the doctor came in, he read the form I had filled out and he clapped his hands but I didn't hear anything. He looked surprised. He opened a drawer, pulled out a bag and took a little hammer and tuning fork from it. He put the tuning fork close to my ear and hit it with the hammer. I did hear something. "I heard that," I said. "Just a little." He went to the other side and did it again. I thought I heard it but wasn't sure. He picked up a tool with a light on the end of it and stuck it into my ear and looked through it like a periscope. He moved it around. That hurt. I could feel his breath on my neck. He went around to the other side and did the same thing. Then he wrote down on a sheet of paper and showed it to me. "You heard a very loud noise?"

I said yes, but wasn't about to tell him that I had been chased by the Indian navy and that they had attacked my submarine with depth charges. He wrote something else and tore a little sheet off a pad. Then he wrote on the other sheet again. "Prescription for steroid drops. Ears are damaged but will heal. Put drops in twice a day until gone."

"Thank you," I said. "How long will it take to get better?"

He raised two fingers, then three, and tossed his head to one side.

"Two or three days?"

He shook his head.

"Weeks?"

He nodded. Shoot.

I paid for the visit. It was only the same as twenty dollars in Canada, which was really cheap. The nurse drew a small map to show me where to buy the eardrops. I met the boy outside. Suddenly I had an idea and ran back inside and asked the nurse to come to the door for a moment. She frowned but came. I asked her to ask the boy his name and write it down for me. She shook her head. No. She wouldn't do it! I couldn't believe it. What the heck was wrong with her?

I let Hollie out and we walked away. Now I was hungry. "Are you hungry?" I asked the boy. He nodded. "Good. Me too. Let's go find a restaurant."

We found three restaurants but none of them would let the boy in. They saw him standing there staring at the ground in shame and they shook their heads at me. Holy smokes! So we went back to the Chinese fishing nets. There were people baking fish and onions and selling them. And there was more of that delicious drink. I bought a whole bunch of everything and we sat down by the nets and ate it, and man it was good. Suddenly my first mate came gliding out of the sky and landed beside us, probably because he saw us eating. The boy was startled to see a seagull come so close to us, and couldn't believe it when the seagull let Hollie sniff its feathers. I explained that Seaweed was part of my crew.

The boy twisted his face up in confusion. What did I mean?

I smiled. Boy, was he in for a surprise.

Chapter Five

I FOUND THE PHARMACY, bought the eardrops, turned my head sideways and squeezed them into my ears. It tickled so badly my eyes watered and my toes curled in my sneakers. The liquid bubbled and crackled in my head, with the sound of a ship sinking under water, a sound that I hated. I waited till the bubbling stopped, then we walked all around old Kochi.

It was an interesting place. If the polar ice cap ever melted, Kochi would be one of the first places to disappear under water. It was completely flat, yet you couldn't see far because of all the buildings and houses. Some of the old houses had colourful arches and little bridges and dark alleys between them, and some had sculpted faces that stared down at you from a timeless past. Some were just flat and boxy, with clotheslines wrapped around them, which reminded me of houses in Newfoundland, and in the Arctic, where they were so plain. And some of the houses were completely rundown, like the abandoned warehouses, leaning over as if they would fall, but not falling.

But there was also a neighbourhood that was very wealthy, where the houses were large and fancy, like in Hollywood, or some rich place like that. There were high iron gates to keep people out, beautiful lawns, enormous gardens, and little houses beside the big houses that were just for decoration. There were expensive cars there too, and they were driven by chauffeurs. I was amazed to see such a rich neighborhood so close to the poor areas, but I didn't get to see much of it because the boy was too afraid to walk there. He shook his head desperately to tell me that he was not allowed. Was he not even allowed to walk down the street? No! He made gestures of hitting and kicking. He would get beaten? Yes. But why? He pointed to his bare arm. I was confused. He would get beaten just for walking there? Yes. He took my hand and tried to pull me away. Okay, I said. And we turned away.

Since we couldn't seem to eat in a regular restaurant together, I went into a store and bought groceries to bring back to the warehouse for later. The boy waited outside with Hollie and Seaweed while I chose packages of Indian food that looked good. The pictures on the boxes showed mothers happily serving food to happy families. I was curious to find out what it tasted like. I also bought fresh oranges, bananas, a melon, grapes, bread, cookies, milk and juice. I had rice on the sub already.

On the way back to the warehouse we ate a whole box of cookies and drank a bottle of juice. It was twilight when we approached the channel where the drain was. We sat on the bank and waited until dark. Then, when we were sure no one could see us, we pushed open the grate and climbed through the tunnel. Seaweed flew up to the roof. Dark tunnels were not his thing.

Once we were inside the warehouse, I said to the boy, "Now, I have to show you something. Do you know what a submarine is?"

In the light of the flashlight he shook his head. No? Oh boy.

"Okay. Do you know that there are boats that go under water?"

He thought about it for a moment, then nodded.

"Good. Well, I have one of those. That's where I live, with Hollie and Seaweed. And that's how we travel around. Do you understand?"

He looked like he was trying really hard to understand, but he didn't. He shook his head.

"Well, let me show you. Would you like to see our submarine?"

He nodded excitedly.

"Okay. Follow me."

I went towards the boathouse door, and he followed me. I

pulled open the door and shone the flashlight in. At a glance there was nothing there, but I could see the flat circle in the water which was the top of the hatch. "Be careful where you step because the wood is really old here. Can you hold the flashlight and point it right there?" I handed it to him then climbed down onto the hatch and opened it. I looked up and saw the flashlight pointed at my face and the dark outline of the small figure behind it. "This is our submarine. Do you want to see inside? Just wait a minute; I'll be right back." I couldn't tell what his answer was. I went in and turned on the emergency lights and pumped air into the tanks to surface completely. I came out and reached up for Hollie and brought him inside. Then, I came back for the groceries.

When I came out again, the boy was ready. He handed me the flashlight, took my hand and jumped onto the hull. He poked his head into the hatch and looked down, filled with wonder. I could tell he was afraid but his curiosity was greater. I think we were the same that way. I showed him where to hold onto the ladder and climb inside.

Hollie was excited to have a visitor in the sub. He ran to his corner, grabbed his ball, brought it over to the boy and dropped it at his feet. As distracted, nervous, and filled with wonder as the boy was, he bent down, picked up the ball and patted Hollie.

I showed him around the sub. I didn't think his eyes could have opened any wider. He was especially interested in the observation window in the floor, and the periscope, even though he couldn't see anything through it in the dark. I showed him the bicycle, the engine, the batteries, and explained that we had been chased by the Indian navy and that the submarine wasn't working right and I had to fix it before we could go anywhere else. He nodded as though he understood everything I was saying, but I didn't think that he did. How could he?

While I made supper, the boy sat by the observation window and played with Hollie. I was surprised how quickly he seemed comfortable here. He had a lot of energy for Hollie, which was nice; Hollie loved getting attention from other people.

I cooked rice and mixed three of the packages with water until they turned into bright green, yellow and red sauces. Then I mixed yogurt, water and sugar together and whipped it up into a drink called a lassie—I read the instructions in my guide book. I cut up the melon and put it on a plate with grapes. Then I laid everything out in bowls and plates on the floor in the bow. Hollie sniffed at everything but I fed him a can of dog food in his dish by the engine room.

We sat and ate. The boy ate without taking a drink. I had to take a drink after every bite because the sauces were so hot and spicy it was like lighting matches in my mouth. My whole body felt hot and my forehead broke into a sweat. Then I had to make more lassie to cool my mouth down. Indian food was tasty but it was like eating fire.

After supper I dug out my chess set. I wanted to see if he could play. He couldn't. Would he like to learn? Yes. Great.

It wasn't easy to teach someone to play chess when they

couldn't ask you questions. Considering that, he learned amazingly fast. He was so fascinated with the game and especially that all the players moved differently and had different powers. We spent a few hours at it, while Hollie lay beside us and watched. Once we started yawning I told the boy he was welcome to sleep inside the sub on a sleeping bag if he wanted to. He nodded emphatically. I told him I had to turn the light off to save power but would light a candle that would burn through the night. When the sun came up I would get busy fixing the batteries.

As I lay in my cot and waited to fall asleep, I thought of how different life was in India. In Canada, no one would let a ten-year-old boy live by himself. Clinics and banks wouldn't refuse to let him inside. What if he got really sick? What then? Here, he wasn't allowed in stores, so how could he buy food and clothes? And where would he get the money anyway? How will he be able to get a job when he is older if he isn't in school now learning to read and write? It was lucky at least that India was so warm. He would never survive a Canadian winter living the way he did. No one would. And yet he seemed kind of happy, strangely enough. He seemed happy to be alive. How different the world was here, I thought, as I drifted off to sleep.

I woke and saw the boy asleep with an arm around Hollie. Even though Hollie was awake I could see that he didn't want to disturb the boy by moving. It was as if Hollie knew somehow that the boy was as he had once been himself—orphaned and alone in the world. I put the kettle on for tea, turned the emergency lights on and started examining the batteries. I couldn't see anything wrong with them, but Ziegfried had taught me not to trust the look of things, to examine them thoroughly, and so I did.

I checked all the wires and all the connectors. Everything had been so well constructed and was designed to absorb lots of bouncing and banging around it was hard to believe anything was broken. And then I found it. Ziegfried had built a relay switch between the batteries and the rest of the sub. Inside the relay switch was a row of fuses. One of the fuses was burnt out. The explosions must have caused the batteries to surge and overwhelm the fuse. That was it. That's all it took to shut the sub down.

Fortunately for me, Ziegfried had stocked the sub with extra parts for everything, including extra fuses. But when I went looking through the parts drawer I couldn't find them. I had a vague memory of having brought the fuses along when I went into the Sahara Desert to fix an engine the year before. I also had a vague memory of having forgotten to bring them back. Shoot! Ah, well, that just meant I'd have to pull the fuse out, find an electrician's shop and buy another one to replace it. Surely there was an electrician's shop in Kochi?

Nope, there wasn't. But there were some in Ernakulum, the city across the harbour. And we could take a ferry there. I learned that after the boy woke up and we went out for fried fish and more of that delicious cinnamon tea, which, according to my guide book, was called chai, now my new favourite drink.

Seaweed was waiting for us when we came out of the sewer drain. We strolled along the road beneath a cloudless sky towards the Chinese fishing nets and our breakfast. I asked the boy if he was allowed on the ferry. Yes. Great. We greeted the men at the road stands, bought grilled fish, onions and chai, then sat and ate while we watched the Chinese nets scoop fish out of the sea. Certainly if there were any place in the world that made homelessness tolerable this was it. Some Pacific islands wouldn't be too bad either.

The ferry ride was a treat. It was a noisy old boat with an exposed engine in the centre that whined and coughed and blew smoke all the way across the harbour. Every inch of the boat was filled with people squashed together like sardines. The boy and I stood on the bow and had a spectacular view of the harbour and its incredible number and variety of vessels. Hollie sat in the tool bag on my back. Seaweed was up in the air somewhere.

From the far side of the harbour I could see where the naval base was. I also saw navy helicopters taking off and landing nearby. Boy was I ever foolish trying to sneak in here in the daytime.

Ernakulum was a modern city, but nothing like a Canadian city. It was very noisy and busy, with way too much traffic for the streets, and man, what strange traffic! There were cars, trucks and buses—new ones and old ones, and some that were painted bright pink, red, yellow, green and purple. The buses were jam-packed with people. You never saw so many people on a bus in Canada. It would be illegal there. There were also taxis everywhere—four-wheeled ones, three-wheeled ones and rickshaws. There were men hauling wooden carts piled high with wood, metal, boxes and burlap sacks. I even saw one filled with dead carcasses. In the middle of all of this, unbelievably, cows were wandering around like it was nobody's business! Somehow the traffic was racing around the cows without hitting them. I didn't see how it was possible, but it was. There was also garbage everywhere. There seemed to be no garbage pick-up whatsoever.

Once we got away from the busier streets we found smaller, quieter streets where all the working shops were—the garages, wood-workers, tanners, shoemakers, rice sellers, spice sellers, paper sellers, tinsmiths, printers, plumbers and electricians. Most of these shops were in two- or three-storey buildings and were squeezed into tight spaces. It was easy to walk around here and there was a lot to see. We passed a sewing machine shop that had dozens of old-fashioned sewing machines that you would only see in museums back in Canada, the ones that you pedal and that don't use electricity. These were brand new. They were still making them in India. Cool. Then I saw a bicycle shop with old-fashioned bikes and they were brand new too. Oh, they were so beautiful!

"Let's go in here," I said. But a clerk met us at the door and wouldn't let the boy in. Oh, yah, I forgot. So we stood at the window and looked in. But the clerk didn't like that either and came out and made a fuss, so we left.

Finally, we stood in front of an electrician's shop. Through the window I saw a stern-looking man sitting at the counter reading a newspaper. "Just wait here, okay?" I said to the boy. "I'll be right back." And I went into the shop. I walked up to the counter with Hollie on my back and pulled the fuse out of my pocket. Before I could say anything, the man spoke to me and made an angry gesture towards the boy.

"I told him to stay outside already," I said. "I just want a fuse."

The man frowned furiously, left his counter and went out to the boy. I started after him, to make sure he wouldn't hurt the boy. To my surprise, he put a smile on his face and invited him inside his shop very graciously. I was confused. As they passed me, the man spoke to me sternly but I couldn't hear him. "I can't hear," I said, pointing to my ear.

He stared dumbly for a second, then grabbed a pen and paper from the counter and scribbled something on it and raised it to my face. It read, "We are all God's children." Then he frowned at me again. Oh boy.

Chapter Six

I LEFT THE ELECTRICIAN'S shop with three valuable things: a fuse for the sub (actually two); the boy's name written on a piece of paper (it was Radji); and a valuable lesson—not to let the actions of others teach me how to act, especially when their actions are unkind. It wasn't a lesson wasted on me.

I was so happy to learn Radji's name. It amazed me what a difference it made knowing a person's name. No wonder we all had names. It wasn't just so that we could tell each other apart; a name gave someone an identity, a whole personality. It was something we each owned, and no one could take it away from us. If someone refused to recognize our name, they were in a way trying to deny our right to exist. I found that fascinating.

We went down a few more streets and I enjoyed looking in the shop windows because the shops were so different from shops in Canada, where most things were now sold in huge department stores and malls. Here you would find little shops that sold just one thing, such as hoses, or vacuum cleaners, or notebooks, or spices. The spice shops were wonderful. You always knew when you were approaching a spice shop because you would smell it first, although sometimes you couldn't because of the garbage and open sewers that created some pretty awful smells. In India it was either feast or famine for your nose.

And then we came upon a chess shop and Radji stopped and stared in the window. There were glass chess sets, metal ones, stone ones, wooden ones and plastic ones. Radji stared in wonder. He was hooked already. He pulled the bill I had given him out of his pocket and stared at it. I peeked at the price tags on the chess sets. They were way too much money for him. He said something and put his money back. I wished I knew what he had said.

A little while later we saw a small department store that sold a little bit of everything, even groceries. Radji seemed very keen to go in.

"Is there something you want to buy?"

He nodded.

"Okay, let's try."

So, we climbed the steps and started in. But a big man with a big round face took a close look at Radji, and Radji dropped his head and wouldn't look up. The man shook his head sharply and pointed us out. I felt like punching him in his big round face. But we went out. Then we found another store and tried again but the same thing happened. Then we tried again and again, but every time Radji had to look somebody in the face he would drop his eyes, turn red and look as if he had just stolen someone's wallet and been caught. I had been taught always to look people in the eye, but this was something Radji simply couldn't do. Not only his face looked guilty; his whole body did. His shoulders fell forward and his hands went flat against his sides and he looked as if he wanted to curl up into a ball. Again, it made me think of a small dog in a pack of bigger dogs. I had seen smaller dogs dominate bigger dogs, but they had to be really confident to do it. Radji didn't seem to have a scrap of confidence. Combined with bare feet and rags for clothes it wasn't hard to tell that he was an Untouchable.

But then I learned something else about Radji, something really interesting: he never seemed to get discouraged. He knew they weren't going to let him in but he never stopped trying. After a while I became more interested in watching Radji's calm reaction to getting refused than I was in watching the anger and disapproval of the shop clerks. And then, I had an idea. I went into a shop and bought a pair of plain white sneakers, a long-sleeved top, a pair of sunglasses and a small hat in one shop. All together it cost me about $1.75 in Canadian money. I suggested to Radji that he put the things on and see what would happen. So he did. At the next shop, they didn't even look at him; they just let him in. He looked kind of funny to me but he was happy to have the disguise.

When he came out of the store he was carrying a tube of cream that looked like toothpaste. I was curious. What did he want so badly that he would go to so much trouble for it? "What's that?" I asked. He handed me the tube and I looked at it but still didn't understand. Then he pointed to a poster on the window of the department store. I stared at it but it took awhile for me to understand what it was. Then my face fell. It was a skin-whitening cream. The poster guaranteed that your skin would lighten in colour by three degrees in just a few weeks of using this cream. The poster showed a ruler with three inches highlighted. It also featured a happy Indian family laughing and playing together. Their skin was white.

Radji didn't waste time putting the cream on his skin. He did it right away. He covered his arms, legs, face, belly, hands and feet. He asked me to help him with his back. I thought it was crazy but I didn't want to tell him that. I carried his hat, shoes, shirt and sunglasses. He stopped to look at his reflection in shop windows all the way back to the ferry. "I don't think it works that fast," I said.

While we waited for the ferry I looked at the local newspapers. There were some in Hindi and some in English—the two official languages of India. I bought an English one and sat on the bank to read it. I was surprised to see the same advertisement for Radji's skin cream on the back of the paper. I was even more surprised to find a picture of two navy ships at sea and a caption that read, "Navy Still Searching for Sunken Sub." I read the article with fascination. They thought they had located the sunken submarine by sonar but when they sent divers down it turned out to be an old sunken barge. Now they believed the sub had only been crippled by their attack and probably went a short distance before it sank for good. There had been no more sightings of it, but the navy was staying vigilant. Wow! I also read that, although the Indian navy did have a submarine, it was being refitted and would not be taking part in this search. That was good to know. As we rode the ferry back to Kochi, I saw two navy patrol boats heading out to sea. Boy, would we ever have to be careful leaving here.

On the other side of the ferry there was a small pizzeria, so I bought a pizza and we ate it on the way back to the warehouse. It was so good. Seaweed dropped in and he and Hollie shared the crusts. I didn't think Radji saw anything on the way back but the skin of his arms and legs because he kept checking them constantly. A few times he showed his arm to me with a questioning look on his face. I just shrugged. I knew he was hoping that if he just whitened his skin his whole life would change. I didn't know how to tell him that it was quite a bit more complicated than that. The advertisements made you think it wasn't. Of course Radji hadn't read them because he couldn't read. I asked him if he could and he shook his head. But he could understand the pictures. I wondered what he was really looking for, white skin, or a happy family?

Back at the sub I replaced the fuse and we had power once again. Yay! It was quite a testament to Ziegfried's construction that we had been attacked by the Indian navy and suffered only a blown fuse. I couldn't wait to share that with him, and with Sheba, who was like a mother to me (and a queen to Ziegfried), and whose home was my home when we weren't at sea. But of course I had to wait for my hearing to improve enough to use the short-wave radio. I also wanted to call my sister, Angel. They would be worried about me. Then it occurred to me—maybe I could get Radji to talk for me, just to let everyone know I was okay.

First we played chess. I had never seen anybody study the board so intensely. Radji stared at every character is if he were expecting them to start moving by themselves. And whenever I made a move, he studied my face closely to figure out why. I thought maybe I should tell him it was just a game. But it seemed to mean a lot more to him than that. My grandfather had taught me how to play, and he followed the principle of "showing no quarter," which meant he never let me win. He said I would learn faster that way, and whenever I did win, it would be a true win. Now, I always beat my grandfather in chess (mostly because he doesn't like to take risks) and I show him no quarter. Ziegfried is an expert player and I play with him whenever I feel like taking a beating. He is absolutely merciless and I never last more than ten moves.

My only strategy is to try to distract him, as in the time I asked him the difference between a water buffalo and a bison.

"What?" he said.

"The difference between a water buffalo and a bison."

"Just a minute." He twisted his mouth to one side. "Horns."

"What?"

"A water buffalo has longer horns. Checkmate!"

But Radji was only ten, and I was sixteen. Still, I felt I should tell him that I would give him no quarter, and then explain what it meant. And so I did. Then he said something to me, and I tried really hard to read his lips. I'm pretty sure he said, "I won't give you any either."

He learned very quickly. He played as if it were life and death, and yet when he lost, over and over and over again, he didn't get discouraged. He only wanted to play more.

Before bed I turned on the short-wave radio and attempted to call Ziegfried. Radji sat beside me as I spoke into the transmitter. I asked him to listen for a deep man's voice. The man would say my name—Al. I started speaking, explaining that I could talk but not hear, and that my friend, Radji, would listen for me. Radji listened intensely, but for a long time there was nothing. I think he would have stayed up all night trying but I was getting tired. Suddenly his face lit up and I saw him speak into the transmitter. "Is it Ziegfried?" I asked. Radji asked, then nodded. So, I started talking again and explained that I had an infection in my ears but was taking drops for it and it would clear up very soon. Everything else was fine. I hoped everyone at home was great, and would he please contact my sister for me and explain why I hadn't called? Radji listened to Ziegfried's response, then spoke back to him again and smiled. I could tell he was excited to speak into the short-wave, and I was grateful for his help. Going without hearing was extremely inconvenient, and I would be glad when it returned. By then, I would be ready to leave Kochi. That would mean saying goodbye to Radji though, and I wasn't looking forward to that. But that was the way Hollie, Seaweed and I travelled—we met people, made friends, and moved on. It was what we were used to. What I couldn't know, of course, was what it might mean to Radji.

Chapter Seven

THE EARDROPS WORKED pretty well. After just a few days I could hear loud sounds, but not quiet ones. Each day my hearing got better. I started to hear Radji, without understanding him yet. He sounded like a baby goat, he spoke so quietly. But I heard him shout once, when he took my knight in chess. He didn't know at the time that it was a trap to get his queen. I thought I detected a little frustration in him when I took his queen, but maybe I was just imagining it because that's how I would have felt. It didn't feel right to be so ruthless with him. He must have thought I was mean. On the other hand, watching how quickly he learned to play chess made me think that he could probably learn to do anything because he was so determined and patient. Each day he put on his skin cream and rubbed it in carefully. Then he shoved his arms under my nose with a questioning look on his face. I looked closely at his skin. It seemed a little bit whiter to me, although it was also kind of blotchy. It didn't look as though it was going to last. I nodded and shrugged. "I guess it's working." He grinned with pride.

We spent a few more days walking around Kochi and Ernakulum, and I stocked up on fresh groceries. I bought potatoes, onions, carrots, squash, oranges, bananas and pineapple. I also bought as much yogurt as I could fit into my little fridge, and some that I froze. I had started making lassies with bananas and with cinnamon. I also bought a bunch of fried fish and squeezed it into my freezer.

Finally the time came for us to leave. I managed to open one of the windows of the warehouse and coax Seaweed in, then shut it. I prepared everything so that we could leave in the middle of the night. I planned to pedal out of the channel, then surface and head out to sea on engine power with the lights on so that we would resemble a small boat in the dark and on radar. If we were spotted I would dive as deeply as possible and pedal as I had done before. Then I would find a ship to hide beneath, but this time I would look at it first.

It was difficult to say goodbye to Radji. We had become good friends in a short time, even though he was only ten and even though I had hardly heard him speak. I thought he was a wonderful person, and I told him so. He surprised me by how well he accepted that we were leaving, because I knew he had also become very fond of Hollie. He never cried. Or if he did, I didn't see it. It was dark when we were ready to leave. Seaweed and Hollie were settled in their spots around the observation window. I went back inside the warehouse with Radji to say goodbye at his sleeping place in the wall; that way he wouldn't have to make his way back there alone in the dark. I gave him a hug and told him, "Never let anyone stand in the way of your dreams. No one! That is what I believe and that is how I live my life." I couldn't see his eyes clearly but he nodded his head with conviction, and I knew that he understood me. As a parting gift, I gave him my chess set. He hugged me again. Then I left.

I made my way carefully back through the warehouse to the boathouse, then climbed into the sub, shut the hatch and submerged. I felt awful inside. I missed Radji already. I didn't know what kind of life he was going to have. He deserved so much more than he had, but I couldn't give it to him. I certainly couldn't take him with me; it was way too dangerous, especially around here, especially right now. And so I left, as I knew I had to. But I felt sad.

I pedalled out of the boathouse, rose to periscope depth, turned to port and pedalled out of the channel. When we turned the corner I came in close to shore, near where the ferries docked, surfaced in the dark, started the engine and headed out to sea. For anyone watching on radar we would probably look like a boat heading out early to fish. I put our lights on too. You would have to come pretty close to know we were a submarine. And if you did, we would disappear.

Seaweed was sitting perfectly still and was probably asleep. Hollie was chewing his rope, which normally I could hear but couldn't right now. The ringing in my ears was almost gone though. It just felt like they needed a good cleaning. Suddenly, Hollie jumped up and ran back into the stern. It didn't surprise me; it was a game of hide-and-seek he had played with Radji. Radji would sneak off and hide in the stern and Hollie would find him. Hollie loved it.

"I'm sorry, Hollie. Radji's not here anymore."

But Hollie persisted. I got up and went into the stern. "He's not here. See?" I opened the door to the engine compartment. Hollie took a look, then stared at me, disappointed. "I'm sorry. He's not here." I threw his ball into the bow and he went after it. I returned to the control panel and watched the radar screen.

As before, there was lots of traffic. But this time I wasn't looking for a place to hide or wait, I wanted to get out of here. Maybe the safest thing was to keep pretending to be a sailboat. But it was painfully slow. Besides, the sun would be up soon and we'd have to submerge then anyway. I bet the navy was keeping an eye on the water with helicopters. They would spot us easily if we were anywhere near the surface. I decided to crank up our engine speed now to twenty knots and sail as far as we could before we'd have to go under and slow down.

With the hatch open, and even with the engine running, I

would normally have heard a helicopter in the air above us. But now I couldn't. If there was one, I would never know. And there was one! I only found out because I had climbed the portal to pee over the side. I saw the lights in the sky and I saw a floodlight almost tracing our wake. "No!" I yelled, and climbed in, pulled the hatch down and sealed it, then ran for the controls and hit the dive switch.

Had they seen us? I didn't know. Maybe. They must have known we were there if they were out at night with their search lights on. Man, they were taking this search really seriously. Now I couldn't risk sailing even on battery power. I'd have to go down deep and pedal. Shoot!

So, I submerged to three hundred feet and climbed up on the bike. I kept sonar on to know where we were going and make sure we didn't run into the bottom. At least I knew there wouldn't be a submarine after us. And there hadn't been any ships close enough to pick up our sonar when we went down, so I felt confident we were hidden enough to use it. I sighed. We were going so slowly now. But at least we were going. As much as I liked Kochi, I didn't want to be stuck there forever. I felt badly for Radji though. I wondered if he had gone to sleep in his little hiding spot in the wall. Then Hollie jumped up and went into the stern again. He wanted to play that game.

"I can't play now, Hollie, I have to pedal."

But he wouldn't give up. He came back and stood beside me and stared at me.

"He's not there," I said. But Hollie kept staring. "Oh, for

Heaven's sake!" I jumped off the bike and followed Hollie into the stern. This time he stood at the compartment where we kept our root vegetables. It was the one compartment we didn't heat. I opened the door and turned on the light. "See? There's nothing here but bags of potatoes and carrots and onions." But Hollie went to the pile of potato bags and barked. "You're being silly, Hollie, barking at potatoes." And then I saw a foot sticking out beneath one bag, and I recognized the white sneaker. It was Radji.

At first I thought maybe I was dreaming. I couldn't figure out how he could possibly have snuck inside. Then I realized that he must have run past me in the dark of the warehouse and I never heard him. No wonder he hadn't been too upset about us leaving him behind; he had no intention of being left behind.

"Radji!" He didn't move. "Radji! I can see your foot." The foot disappeared beneath the potatoes. I was about to give him a blast. I was about to tell him how he should never have come because it was too dangerous, and how I couldn't look after him and what was he hoping to find by coming with us anyway? And I wondered how to take him back. But I sure didn't want to go back there now. Then I remembered telling him not to let anyone stand in the way of his dreams. As I stood and stared at the pile of potatoes concealing him, I realized that he hadn't, and I had to smile. Radji had done to me exactly what I was trying to do to the India navy. He had outsmarted me.

Chapter Eight

"CAN YOU SWIM?"

"Yes."

"Are you sure?"

"Yes."

"Can you hold your breath under water?"

"Yes."

"How long?"

"I'm not sure. Maybe ten minutes."

"Nobody can do that. See how long you can hold it now. Take a deep breath."

Radji took a deep breath, shut his mouth and shut his eyes. I watched the clock. His face slowly turned red and started to shake. Then his mouth burst open. "How long was that?" he asked, gasping.

I could understand him now if I stared at his mouth when he spoke. "Not bad. Forty-seven seconds. It's harder under water."

"I do it better under water."

"Hmmm. Radji, the reason I didn't take you in my sub is because it really is dangerous."

"I know. I am not afraid."

"I know you are not afraid. That's not the point. I have a rule about not taking passengers because it's so dangerous. Right now the Indian navy is searching for us. That's why I can't hear properly—they found us once before and shot explosives at us and almost killed us."

"But you escaped them."

"Yes, we escaped them, but we almost didn't."

"But you did. You will always escape them. And now I can help you."

I stared into his determined face and he stared back at me. For a moment, all we did was stare. Then I took a deep breath. So he took a deep breath. I took another one and sighed. "Oh man . . . do you want some tea?"

We had a cup of tea and shared an orange. Then I climbed up on the bike and continued pedalling while Radji sat with Hollie and patted him. I pedalled for two hours and watched Radji fall asleep. It was the middle of the night. But now I wanted to surface to see if we had been followed. If we hadn't, we could continue on battery power, which would be so much faster. And then, when we were further away, I could go to sleep too. But I couldn't turn on the batteries if anyone was close enough to listen with sonar. And I was nervous about surfacing in the path of a ship. Normally I would hear the engines of a ship before we were too close, but I couldn't hear them now unless they were about to run us over. So, I stood over Radji and considered waking him. I hated to wake him, but this is what he was asking for. He should see it for what it was. I reached down and shook him. "Radji! Radji!"

He opened his eyes, raised his head in confusion and looked around as if he had forgotten where he was. I knew that feeling. "Radji, I need your ears. We're going to surface. I need you to listen for engine sounds. Can you do that?"

He rubbed his eyes and nodded.

"Good. We have to be very quiet, okay? All you have to do is listen. If you hear anything, nod your head. If you don't hear anything when I raise my hand like this, shake your head. Okay?"

"Okay."

"Good. Let's go."

I pumped air into the tanks and we started up. If there were ships up there waiting for us I wanted Radji to be awake anyway. This was exactly the kind of danger I never wanted to share with anyone else, but that decision had been taken out of my hands.

I stared at the depth gauge, watched Radji's face, and kept

my hand on the dive switch. He was listening carefully. When we reached seventy-five feet I let some water into the tanks and we stopped rising. I raised my hand. Radji shook his head. "Are you sure?" I whispered. He nodded. I pumped more air into the tanks and we came closer to the surface and I raised the periscope and looked. There was nothing there. I turned it 360 degrees, twice, and saw nothing. What a relief. I was about to surface and turn on radar when Radji asked if he could look.

"Sure."

I grabbed a coil of rope for him to stand on and showed him where to hold his hands and how to look. He stared into the periscope the same way he stared at chess pieces, with complete concentration. Slowly he turned it around. He had to stand on his tiptoes to hang onto it.

"There's nothing to see now because it's dark and there's nothing out there, but in the morning you'll be able to see waves and the horizon, and maybe a passing ship."

Then he said something but I couldn't hear it.

"What?"

He turned to me and said, "What's that shadow out there?"

"Shadow? What shadow? I didn't see a shadow. Let me look."

He jumped down and I looked. As I traced along the dark line of the horizon I saw where the line was broken and the darkness was a little darker. It looked like a shadow but was actually the silhouette of a ship. It was probably five or six miles away. Its lights were out, which was illegal of course, and was only happening because it was a navy ship hoping to catch us. If I had broken the surface with the portal and turned on our radar, they would have located us instantly, and the chase would be on again. But Radji had spotted them. I pulled the periscope down and let water into the tanks. We went back down to three hundred feet and I climbed back onto the bicycle. Radji curled up on the sleeping bag with Hollie.

"Good job, Radji."

"Thank you."

Two hours later I woke him to do it all over again. This time there were no ships. Radar confirmed it. I opened the hatch, turned on the engine and cranked it up. I wanted to get as far from here as we could while the going was good. The sun was coming up. Seaweed climbed the ladder and jumped into the air. Radji asked if he could come up too.

"Of course. But you must never climb out of the portal without putting on this harness first, okay? Will you promise?"

"I promise."

"Good. Here, take the binoculars. You can look around. If you see any ships, let me know right away, okay?"

"Okay."

I went back inside. It was strange having Radji on board. I didn't know what to think of it really. He had certainly saved us a lot of trouble spotting that ship. And he was great company for Hollie. But what was I going to do with him? I really had no idea. I'd have to ask Ziegfried and Sheba. Maybe they would know. Gosh, I was sleepy now. Hot chocolate would go down well. "Hey, Radji? Do you want some hot chocolate? . . . Radji? . . . Radji?"

There was no answer. I figured I couldn't hear him. I waited for a second for him to come down. He didn't. I went to the bottom of the ladder and looked up. He wasn't there. "Radji?" I bolted up the ladder. But he was gone.

I rushed inside and shut off the engine. I flew up the ladder and scanned the water in our wake but didn't see anything. "Radji! . . . Radji!" I yelled as loudly as I could and listened hard but couldn't hear anything. I had to think fast. How long had he been up here by himself? Five minutes? Ten minutes? No, not that long. It was maybe only a minute or two. Should I turn on the engine and go back or just dive in the water and swim for him? The sun was just clearing the horizon and the water was dark blue. I couldn't see much below the surface. "Act!" I yelled at myself. I jumped down inside, flipped the engine switch on, turned the sub around and headed back. I found our wake and steered into the center of it. "Radji!"

I climbed down onto the hull and leaned over the bow as we cut through the water. I stared at the water, looking for anything, any bubbles or slight discolouring. Then, about twenty-five feet in front of us I saw one of Radji's white sneakers. I jumped inside and shut off the engine, flew up the ladder and dove over the side. I found him about ten feet under. He wasn't moving but his eyes were open and staring at me. He was concentrating on holding his breath. I grabbed him and pulled him to the surface. The sub bumped into us as it drifted by. Radji gasped for air and started coughing up water. I held onto him with one arm and swam after the sub. It took a long time to catch it.

"I'm sorry," Radji said as I carried him through the water.

"It's okay," I said. "I thought you said you could swim."

"I can, when my feet are touching the bottom."

I laughed nervously. Inside I was fighting back my tears. He had almost drowned. If he had drowned . . . well, I just didn't think I could have lived with that. "Why did you go out without the harness?"

"I dropped your binoculars. I tried to reach them but they sank. I thought you would be angry with me."

He looked at me. "Are you angry with me?"

"No. No, I am not angry."

"I held my breath a really long time."

"I know."

Chapter Nine

I MADE HOT CHOCOLATE and we sat on the floor by the observation window and drank it. Radji was wrapped up in the sleeping bag and Hollie was on his lap. He wasn't cold, he was frightened. I could tell, even though he was good at hiding what he was feeling.

"Where did you come from, Radji?"

He stared over the edge of his cup and the little steam rising out of it. "It's a secret."

"But you must have some family somewhere? *Somebody* must be worried about you?"

He started breathing heavily. "I can tell you my secret if you promise you will never tell anyone."

"I promise I will never tell anyone. I wouldn't anyway."

"I ran away."

"Why did you run away?"

"Because my father beat me."

"Oh."

He said it so matter-of-factly. "But what about your mother? Doesn't she miss you?"

"My father beat my mother too, but she could not run away. I think maybe because I ran away he will not beat her so much. I was the one who made him angry all the time. Then he beat everybody."

He stared at the floor, lost in his thoughts. "When I am older I will go back. Then I will stop my father."

"That's what I would do too."

"But first I need to go to Varanasi."

"Varanasi? Why do you want to go there?"

He looked at me as if I should know why. "Because it is a holy city. The river Ganges flows there. The river is a great goddess. When I bathe in the river, I will be cleansed of my sins and my life will change."

"But Radji, you are only ten. What sins could you have?"

He looked at me strangely. For a moment I felt as if I were talking to an old man. It was weird. He looked down. "It is another secret. But I cannot tell you this one."

"That's okay. You don't have to tell me. I don't need to know."

What sins could a ten-year-old boy have that would weigh on him so heavily? I couldn't imagine.

We sailed close enough to shore to settle on the bottom at a hundred and fifty feet, shut everything off and went to sleep for the day. As tired as I was, it took me a little while to fall asleep because Radji was crying out in his sleep. I couldn't understand what he was saying but it sounded like he was pleading with someone, as if he were trying to make them stop. It was disturbing.

It was almost twelve hours later when we woke, rose to the surface and opened the hatch. The moon was full and close to the earth. It looked like a giant yellow saucer. The radar screen was clear. My guidebook said the southwest coast of India was famous for long, sandy beaches. I figured we could all use a good run on the beach in the middle of the night. So I cranked up the engine and headed east.

Seventy-five feet from shore, I tossed the anchor in twenty feet and inflated the rubber kayak. We jumped in and paddled the short distance to shore. I used to have a rubber dinghy but lost it in a typhoon. I seemed to have a habit of losing dinghies.

The beach was empty and vast. If there were lights on the water we would see them right away. I told Radji not to leave my side. He was still my ears. Hollie took off like lightning and we chased after him. This, I told Radji, was the nice part of the life of a submariner—going where nobody else could go and waking when everyone else was sleeping. He must have thought anything was better than living in a hole in a wall, or living with a father who beat him. I didn't know why but I had always thought of India as a land of gentle people.

I realized now it was a lot more complicated than that. Everywhere was more complicated than that.

When the sun came up we were back in the sub and approaching Goa, where my friend Cinnamon was from. She had been trapped on a ship and taken far away and ended up joining a circus in the Pacific. She had asked me to take her back here so that she could look for her brother who was also lost, but I said no. I didn't feel confident I could protect her. Now that I was here, I felt badly. But what if she had panicked when we were attacked by the navy? What if her hearing had been damaged forever? I just couldn't handle that responsibility. But I wondered where her brother was now. There weren't just a few kids lost and abandoned in India like Radji, there were probably millions.

Goa had a humongous harbour, like Kochi, and was jampacked with ships. This time I looked much more carefully for navy ships. We came in right behind a huge tanker, at periscope depth, so we could see but wouldn't appear separately on sonar. Her engines were so loud the vibration made our teeth chatter and we laughed out loud. Radji said it sounded like someone put a bucket over his head and beat it with sticks. We had to endure it only for half an hour or so.

Once we were inside the harbour there were many other vessels to hide beneath. There wasn't a naval base here but there was a navy destroyer sitting right in the centre of the harbour like an eagle on top of a tree. Yikes! We had a really good look at her through the periscope as we passed and she made me nervous. I kept so close to the tanker I thought my eyeballs were going to shake out of my head. Radji kept shaking his whole body on purpose—to counteract the shaking from the engines. Then the tanker was met by tugboats and she cut her engines. What a relief!

With the tanker between us and the destroyer I scooted close to the banks of the waterfront. There was a giant barge terminal here. The tanker wasn't coming in for oil but for some kind of mineral. It was really interesting—there were hundreds of self-propelled barges bringing the mineral to the terminal, where it was being loaded onto gigantic tankers. They were then taking it somewhere else, probably around the world.

The whole production made me think of ants. There were carrying ants, loading ants and unloading ants: giant ants for the bigger jobs and smaller ants for the smaller jobs. But I was curious about where the barges were coming from. They weren't going to sea; they were going inland, so there must have been a big river. And why was that destroyer sitting in the middle of the harbour like a big, fat bully? The whole situation gave me that kind of curiosity that just wouldn't go away, and I couldn't think of anything else. I wanted to follow a barge upriver.

I figured it was a good idea anyway: Seaweed wanted out; we needed a place to hide; and I was dying to see what India looked like inland from the coast. So, I steered in under the barges and waited for one to leave. What a bizarre feeling having so many barges overhead, like giant beetles floating on a pond. Each barge was about a hundred feet long. They were old and beaten up. I saw blue smoke spewing from one just before we pulled the periscope down. From underneath the water they sounded like a bunch of sick old men coughing and throwing up.

While waiting we had tea, beans, bread and oranges. I studied the map of India and Radji studied the chess board. He put all the players on and practised moving them around. It made me a tiny bit nervous, which was silly. He was so darned determined and clever, and I didn't want him to beat me. The map showed a couple of rivers emptying into the harbour at Goa. The rivers looked like snakes on the map, the way snakes curve when they slither across the sand.

I wondered how far upriver the barges went. I knew that once we left the harbour and were on a river, there would be no question of anyone tracking us with sonar or radar, and that would be a nice break. But sailing up a river can be tricky, as I had learned a year ago on the St. Lawrence River. On the other hand, anywhere these old barges could go, we could go.

Once I had figured out the routine of how the barges came in, unloaded, then lined up to leave, I moved underneath the first one in line. When it started up like a grumpy old troll and pushed its way out of the terminal, we followed it out.

Chapter Ten

IT AMAZED ME TO NO end that you could make an iron boat—heavy enough to flatten a house if you were to drop it on one—fill it to the brim with rocks and it would still float. But if you threw a single stone into the water it would go straight to the bottom. This was the mystery of displacement. Ziegfried explained it to me many times but I never truly understood the theory. I could sense when something was going to float or sink; that was enough for me.

The barge was as slow as molasses but it cut across the water to where the harbour shrank from massive to small. As the barge disappeared up a river, like a mouse into a hole, we were right behind.

Radji watched through the periscope and I watched on sonar. I trusted him because he did everything with intense concentration. I was guessing the river was flowing against us at a gentle three knots, which shouldn't have been much for a barge to plough through, especially empty, but it went very slowly. Maybe they were trying to save fuel. Or maybe they were just not in a hurry. I think we could have walked faster along the bank.

"Radji? Did you ever go to school?"

"No."

"How come you speak English?"

"That's what my mother spoke to me. And my friends. But I speak better than them. I learned also at Kochi. I tried very hard to learn."

"You did a good job. Did anyone ever try to teach you how to read and write?"

"No."

"Do you want to learn?"

"I am going to learn."

"That's good."

"After I bathe in the Ganges my sins will be forgiven. I will be free and everything in my life will change."

"Oh. Can your mother and father read and write?"

"No. I don't know anybody who can."

"Really?"

"Except you. You can."

"Yes. You will really like reading and writing, Radji. You

are very smart. I can tell. You will learn quickly and be amazed at how interesting it is."

"I know. I used to love reading before."

"Before? What do you mean?"

"In another life. Before this one."

"Another life?"

"Yes."

"Oh."

"In another life I read books and even wrote them."

"How do you know that?"

"Because I feel it. Sometimes when I'm sleeping I remember reading books and writing them."

"Cool. What about chess? Did you play chess in another life?"

"I don't think so. I think this is the first time that I played."

"Well, I think you are going to be very good at that too."

"I hope so. I will try my hardest and give no quarter."

I laughed. "That's good. What do you see through the periscope now?"

"I see the barge. I see trees and grass. I see rice fields. I see people working in the fields. I see . . . a temple."

"Really? Let me see."

Radji jumped down and I looked. It was a small grey temple, like a pyramid, but box-shaped. The rice fields came close to the banks of the river. There were ponds in some of the fields. In one of the ponds I saw something slither across the top of the water. I was pretty sure it was a snake. "Are there snakes here?"

"Yes. There are many snakes."

"Are they dangerous?"

"Yes. Many people die."

I opened my guide book and searched for information on snakes. It said that there are four dangerous snakes in India. Every year about two hundred and fifty thousand people get bitten by them and 20 percent die. Wow. That's fifty thousand people. Every year! Holy smokes! Most of the people who die are field workers. It said that if you get bitten you must find the snake and kill it, then take it with you to a medical centre so that they can identify it and give you the right antidote before you die. Great. "Radji. These fields are dangerous."

"I know. I told you."

"Then why the heck are people working in them? And they have bare feet!"

"There is no other work. They must work or they have nothing to eat."

"But that's crazy!"

"No. You only die when it is your time to die. If it isn't your time, then you won't die. Nothing will change that."

"Hmmm. I don't think I believe that."

"I do."

We followed the barge for about fifteen miles, and that took the rest of the day. We passed several barges going the other way. Loaded and riding with the current they came down the river faster than they went up. The further upriver we went, the narrower it became, and some of the turns were tricky, especially when two barges met. Where our barge finally stopped and turned around, there was a dock with trucks backing onto a ramp and unloading. There were half a dozen barges in line in front of ours. I decided to continue around the next bend, find a spot to surface in the dark, toss the anchor and tie up to something.

I tied up to a tree in a dark corner, underneath some hanging branches. It was out of the way of the barge traffic and a good place to hide. We tried to sleep that night so we could get out and explore the next day, but since we had already been sleeping in the day and travelling at night, it was hard to change back. I was used to it but Radji wasn't. Even though he tried hard to go to sleep I heard him bumping around with Hollie, or thought I did, which told me that my hearing was getting a lot better, which was good, except that I had a lousy sleep. So did Radji. Then, with the early morning light coming up through the observation window, I saw him sitting up with Hollie and studying the chess board.

There are days when, if you knew what was coming, you wouldn't get out of bed. You'd pull up the covers and say, "No thanks." But I always wondered: if you avoided days like that, would they just come the next day anyway?

After a breakfast of porridge and tea and oranges, we climbed out of the sub and left it tied to the tree, with the portal sticking up just a few inches beneath the shadow of the branches. The only traffic on the river was the barges, and there was no way they would ever notice the portal in that corner, especially when they were busy navigating the turn. Some barges went further upstream where there must have been other unloading docks along the river, which meant there were other quarries too. In between the quarries were rice fields, ponds and wooded areas. We had seen them along the way. I figured we could walk in a wooded area and stay clear of the rice fields and ponds.

I took along the tool bag for Hollie but he started on foot. Seaweed was already out and gone. I sure hoped he would be careful around snakes. He had a surprisingly aggressive nature when he was on his own. He would attack and rip apart crabs of all types and sizes and didn't seem to be afraid of anything, except snowy owls in the Arctic. But snowy owls would chase wolves away from their nests. Sometimes I wondered if Seaweed thought he was actually an eagle or an osprey. I would never show him a mirror, just in case.

We left the river and entered a wooded area. The ground was dry and the trees were dusty. Although it was hot already in the early morning, I loved the heat of India. There was a faint smell of spice in the air but I didn't know which one it was. I kept a constant lookout for snakes. Hollie tramped around cautiously. He was cautious when I was cautious. He sniffed with suspicion. He zigzagged in front and behind us when curious items made it impossible for him to resist; otherwise he tramped steadily at my feet. Through the trees I caught sight of a nearby rice field, and the shiny brown limbs of workers there. I wondered if you took an x-ray of the field how many snakes you would find, and where they would be. I supposed you'd have to have such an attitude as Radji had about life and death if you were going to work there. I wouldn't do it. I'd walk to the sea and fish for a living instead, like my grandfather.

We hadn't gone far when Radji had a bit of bad luck. He tripped on a fallen log and twisted his ankle. He said he was all right but I noticed he limped a little after that. I wondered if he tripped because of the sneakers he was wearing, as he was used to going barefoot. But he was attached to them and refused to take them off.

The woods widened and narrowed and widened again before it reached a field that was not a rice field, and we felt comfortable crossing it. Then we crossed a road and entered another wooded area. Beside the road I saw a poster that showed a father tossing a girl up in the air. The poster said, "Save the Girl Child." "What does that mean, Radji? What does it mean . . . save the girl child?"

Radji turned red and stared at the ground.

"What? What's wrong? What's wrong, Radji? Did I say something wrong?"

"No."

"What's upsetting you?"

"It means babies."

"I don't understand."

Radji started breathing very heavily. I was starting to wonder if he had asthma. He took a few deep breaths and spoke with great stress. "Sometimes . . . sometimes people kill their babies if they are girls."

"*What?*"

He was breathing so hard. I didn't want to upset him anymore. "It's okay, Radji. We don't have to talk about it. It's okay. Let's talk about something else. Let's talk about . . . chess."

"Okay."

And so we did. And I was astonished to learn that Radji had fixed the game in his mind so well already that he could talk about the players and their moves and the spaces as if it were all in front of him. Even so, I couldn't stop wondering what he meant about killing babies. But I wouldn't ask him again. I would ask someone else.

Chapter Eleven

EVERY COUNTRY SMELLS different, feels different, and looks different. India was the most beautiful country I ever saw. If you think of a country as being like an animal then India was the animal with the most colour, the softest fur, the shiniest eyes, the sharpest claws, the longest tail, and the prettiest face. She also smelled the nicest . . . and the *worst*. She smelled like cinnamon and sandalwood and the heat of the ground and your own skin. But she also smelled like the sewer, and you learned quickly which way to turn your head. But that was only in the cities. In the country everything smelled wonderful.

India was also the friendliest country to me, but the most

unfriendly to her own people, it seemed. She was the safest in some ways, yet the most dangerous in others. She was dangerous because of the slithering beasts that lay on the ground like shiny pieces of jewelled rope—hidden behind a log or a bush—that would rush away from you like ribbons in the wind, or stand up and strike you with deadly poison.

The snake caught us completely off-guard. We didn't know it was there because it wasn't where snakes are supposed to be. It wasn't in the field. It wasn't near water or rocks or any place to hide. We had stopped in the woods to look at a beautiful bush with flowers on it, and the snake was there. But we couldn't see it. The colour of the snake blended in with the bush so well we thought it was all one. Even Hollie didn't know it was there. But when it came out of the flowers and struck at Radji, I saw it. And even though it happened in an instant I saw the black eyes of the snake as it went past. Then Hollie started barking and the snake recoiled and struck at him. But Hollie jumped back. By then I had raised my stick and I struck at the snake and hit it on its back. It dropped to the ground and raced into the bushes so quickly all we saw was the thin tail for an instant, and it was gone.

It happened so fast and unexpectedly we were all shocked. Two thoughts raced through my head: had Radji been bitten? And, if he had, I must catch the snake and kill it. Radji had jumped a couple of feet off the ground when the snake had struck, but had it bitten him? He had cried out.

"Radji? Are you okay? Did the snake bite you?"

He was breathing heavily and his face was red and wearing a very serious expression. He nodded his head with resignation. "Yes."

"It did? Oh no! Quick! *Quick*! We have to find a clinic or a hospital. We have to find someone to take us there, to drive us. Quick, we have to hurry now!"

But Radji just sat down, crossed his legs and dropped his head. "No. That doesn't matter now. It is my time now."

"*What*? No, it isn't! Don't be silly! We have to get you to a doctor right now, and we'll get you the right antidote and you'll be fine. Come on, let's go!"

But Radji just sat there and shook his head. I bent down. "Let me see." He stretched out his leg and I saw the nasty red marks just above his ankle. I couldn't believe that those two little marks were where a snake had sunk its poison to kill. What a dangerous creature. "Come on! Let's go!"

Radji got to his feet reluctantly. I couldn't believe how resigned he was. He really thought he was dying, and there was nothing we could do about it. But I would never believe that. I wanted him to run with me but he wouldn't. He was walking, but too slowly. "Come on, Radji! Please try harder!"

"But I am tired. And I am dying anyway. Why try harder?"

"Because you are not going to die. We will find a doctor. You are going to be fine."

Radji did not have the will to try because he did not believe there was any point. But I thought he might also be tired because of the snake's venom. And I saw that his leg was already beginning to swell. That frightened me. "Okay, climb onto my back. I'm going to carry you."

Radji dropped his face. He had no will to continue. I pulled off the tool bag and left it on the ground. "Here. Climb up and hold on around my neck." I said it so firmly he obeyed me. I bent down, he held onto my neck, and I slid my hands underneath his knees. Because he was so light I was able to walk quickly. Hollie looked back at the tool bag, then joined us and trotted by my feet.

I walked as quickly as I could and tried to think positively. I would find a road, stop a car and get them to take us to a clinic. Radji would get the antidote and would be fine. By suppertime everything would be okay.

Well, it didn't work like that. We had crossed three roads earlier, but I couldn't seem to find one now. I didn't want to go back because it was so far. There must be one very close to us now. I walked faster. As light as Radji was, it was a lot of work carrying him. I was quickly out of breath and had to slow down a little.

I couldn't find a road! What a horrible feeling it was. There must be a road, but where was it? Radji was growing more tired. His voice sounded sleepy. "Stay awake, Radji! You have to stay awake."

"But I am so tired."

"Yes, but you have to stay awake."

"Will you take me to Varanasi?"

"What?"

"Will you take me to Varanasi? When I die?"

"Radji. You're not going to die."

"Will you take me if I do? And burn my body? Please?"

"Yes, I will take you, but you are not going to die."

"Do you promise?"

He sounded so sleepy now. "Radji!"

"Do you promise?"

"Yes, I promise. Now stay awake!"

His face bumped against my back as we hurried along. It was getting very difficult to keep walking, but I had to. Where was the road?

Finally I saw a sign and found a road. I waved to the first car to stop but it wouldn't. I waved to the next one too, but they wouldn't stop. When the third car came, I stepped in front of it and forced it to stop, but the driver yelled at us and waved his arms angrily, then drove onto the shoulder and went around us. I couldn't believe it. Wouldn't anyone stop? Then a taxi stopped but was filled with passengers already. I yelled to the driver that Radji had a snake bite and asked if we could squeeze in too but he shook his head. He said that there was a clinic just a mile up the road. Then he drove off. I kept walking and trying to stop every car. But no one else would stop. No one.

Walking that mile was the worst experience in my whole life. Radji went to sleep. I couldn't wake him. I felt his leg with my hand and it was swollen. And even though he was so very light, I became exhausted carrying him so far and couldn't go as fast as I wanted to, as I needed to. I felt so awful. And then something else happened that caused me even more anxiety. When I looked behind me, Hollie wasn't there. He was gone. I yelled for him but he never came. Where had he gone? What happened? I started wondering if maybe he had been bitten by the snake, too. I wanted so badly to go back and find him. He would be expecting me to. But . . . I couldn't. I had to get Radji to the doctor.

That was the worst feeling—wanting so desperately to find Hollie but not being able to. I was carrying a boy on my back who was dying. I couldn't stop. I couldn't go back now. It would have to be later. I could only hope later wouldn't be too late. For now I had to keep going. That's all I could do. It was a nightmare.

The road crossed another road, and for a moment I didn't know which way we should go. They looked the same. But the taxi driver never said to turn off, so I kept going straight, although I worried now that it might be the wrong way. It was bringing us closer to the river. I didn't see any houses or towns or anything but fields and woods. My arms and legs were really tired now. Radji was still asleep. I talked to him but he wouldn't wake up. I tried not to think about what might happen. I tried to think just positive thoughts. And then I saw a house, and then I saw a clinic sign. I was so happy. I tried to walk faster. "Hold on Radji! We are almost there."

The clinic was in someone's house. The house was fancy for being out in the country. It was right next to the river and there was a high iron gate all around it. There was a shiny new car sitting in the driveway and a new motorboat beside that. I went up to the gate but found it locked. There was a bell, so I grabbed it with one hand, still holding Radji on my back. I started ringing the bell and didn't stop until an old woman came out of the house and walked over to us. She opened the gate but when she saw Radji on my back she shook her head. I pushed past her and rushed to the house. I banged on the door with my foot until it opened and there was a man in a suit and a white doctor's coat. "What?" he said.

I pushed inside. "It's my friend. He's been bitten by a snake. Please help us."

The doctor looked at Radji and I saw his nose twitch, as if he were smelling him the way an animal would smell another animal. He took a step back. Radji did smell. His clothes smelled like old carpet, his hair smelled a bit like vinegar, and his fingernails were black. He really needed a bath. I wondered when was the last time he had taken one. But where would Radji take a bath?

The doctor's eyes narrowed with suspicion. He frowned and shook his head. My face fell. "Help us! You're a doctor!"

"I cannot help you," he said.

"Yes, you can! You're a doctor."

"I am a doctor but I cannot help you. Go somewhere else."

"You mean you *won't* help us. You can help us but you won't."

Without changing his voice he said, "I cannot help you. Go somewhere else."

I yelled at him. "*Where*? Where are we supposed to go?"

He went to the door, pushed it open and pointed out. "Go."

Funny the things we notice at times like this. I saw the very same advertisement for Radji's skin cream on the wall of the doctor's office. On the counter was an open box of tubes. The doctor was selling it here. "Go," he said. "Across the street there is another clinic. Maybe they will see you there."

He left the room. I rushed outside, went through the gate and looked down the road. There was a group of buildings at the corner. It looked like the edge of a small town. I grabbed hold of Radji's legs tightly and hurried down the road.

I burst into the clinic, saw several people waiting in chairs and a doctor talking to a nurse. They stopped talking and stared at us. I was almost fainting with fatigue now. "He . . . he . . . got a snake bite!"

The doctor put down her chart. "Quickly!" she said. "Come with me."

I followed her to an examining room where she helped take Radji off my back and lay him onto an examining bed. "How long ago?" she asked.

"Umm . . . about forty-five minutes, I think. We were in the woods."

"Where?"

"I don't know. Down the road." I pointed.

"No. I mean, where is the bite?"

"Oh. Here. Above the ankle. His leg is swollen now."

She felt his forehead, lifted his wrist and started counting his pulse.

"Will he be okay?"

She looked at me very sympathetically while she counted his pulse. "We will certainly hope so."

"The doctor across the street wouldn't see us."

"He would see *you*. He wouldn't see him."

She took a magnifying glass and looked at the snake bite very carefully. "Describe the snake to me."

"It happened so fast. It was green and had black and yellow on it, I think. I wanted to try to kill it and bring it here but never had a chance."

"Were they blocks of colour or stripes?"

"Umm . . . I'm not sure. I think maybe they were stripes."

"But you're not sure?"

"I'm sorry. No."

She felt the swelling on his leg, then compared it to his other leg. "Did he fall? Did he hurt his leg in any other way?"

"Yes. He did. He twisted his ankle this morning. I saw him limping a little bit."

She nodded her head. "And was he maybe very tired?"

"Umm . . . yes, I think so. Our sleep had changed. We had been up all night and sleeping in the day, then we changed back."

"Yes. Well, I think I might have good news for you. I think this is not a venomous bite. We don't need to see the snake to diagnose a snake bite anyway. We can tell by the bite. Not all snakes here are dangerous, although many are. I think your friend was bitten by a harmless snake. Painful, yes, but not deadly."

"But what about the swelling?"

She smiled. She was so kind. "Your friend has been walking around on a sprained ankle. That's why it is swollen. Didn't he complain?"

"No, he never complained."

She touched his forehead affectionately. "He's a tough little guy."

"He is." I swallowed hard. "Can you help me? I have to find my dog. Is there any way I can leave my friend here while I go searching for him? Please?"

She touched my arm gently and looked into my eyes. "He can stay here. Go find your dog. We'll keep him safe and let him rest, and when he wakes we'll find something for him to eat."

"Thank you so much." I could barely get the words out of my mouth without bursting into tears. I felt so grateful. Her kindness took me by surprise. The doctor across the street would have let Radji die. But I couldn't think about that now. Hollie was lost in a dangerous place and I had to find him.

Chapter Twelve

HOLLIE WAS AS CAUTIOUS as a wise old man, he really was. He was curious, of course, but didn't take the kinds of risks that many dogs do. He had been the runt of the litter and was thrown from a wharf with a rope around his neck, tied to a stone. So, his start in life was pretty bleak. And yet he carried a lucky star, too, because he had landed in a dory, not the sea, and somehow that dory untethered and drifted free and I found it. Since then, he has travelled around the world in relative comfort. Still, he doesn't ask for much.

I couldn't figure out what had happened to him. Now that I knew that the snake was not poisonous it must have been something else. Had he been spooked by something? But what? I hadn't seen anything. He was with us one minute, gone the next. I had been so preoccupied with Radji I didn't even notice. I ran back to where we had come out of the woods. I checked the ditch all the way. The thought that he might have been struck by a car came to me but I tried not to think that. Images of finding him lying on his side jumped into my head and I had to push them out. When I reached the woods, I started calling his name. I tried to follow exactly the same path but I wasn't sure it was right. I couldn't remember well enough because we had come through in a panic. I thought I would recognize the bush where the snake had bitten Radji but suddenly there were so many of them. I yelled Hollie's name all the way through the woods but there was no sign of him. I felt discouraged. I was worried sick. I just wanted him back. You could keep all the money in the world, I just wanted my dog back.

Maybe I was going the wrong way. I wasn't sure. I just kept going. Eventually I reached the river. Then I discovered I had travelled too far upstream. I ran down to where the sub was and entered the woods again. Now it looked familiar. I found the woods where the snake had been. Then I recognized the bush. Then, I saw the tool bag, and there, curled up inside the bag, was Hollie.

But there was something wrong with him. He didn't bark. He wagged his tail but he didn't get up. "Hollie? Are you okay?" His face was a little swollen. I examined him very closely. I think maybe he had been bitten by the snake too, and it caused his face to swell. The poor thing. I scooped him up in my arms, threw the bag over my shoulder and headed back towards the clinic. I was worried about him but I was so happy I found him.

Back at the clinic Radji was still sleeping. The doctor was so kind she even examined Hollie for me. She said, yes, he had also been bitten, and being such a small dog, a bite in the face by a large snake would cause swelling and take awhile to heal. He would be sore and lethargic for a few days but would heal just fine. She gave me some medication to put in his food that would make him feel better. I held Hollie on my lap and stroked his fur and talked to him while the doctor saw other patients. She even let us stay after the clinic closed while she did her paperwork.

We talked. I asked her about Untouchables. She said things were changing slowly for them, but it was still a very big problem. "Mahatma Gandhi, our first leader, tried to make it better for them. He was a pacifist. He went on hunger strikes for political change. He did so much for our country, but it is very hard to go against so many centuries of tradition. At least Untouchables have legal rights now that they never had before. But there is still violence and discrimination against them. India is a complicated country with many peoples. And we have not only Hindus here; we have Muslims, Sikhs, Buddhists, Christians, and many others too."

Then I asked her about the save-the-girl-child poster. She made a sad face. "It's a program to stop the euthanasia, the killing of baby girls, before and after they are born."

"But why would anyone kill their babies? That doesn't make any sense."

"Girls are more expensive to have in India than boys."

"Why?"

"Because families have to provide a dowry for them when they marry, and that's expensive. And the other thing is that parents expect to be looked after by their sons in their old age. So, if a family has only girls, they have to pay money for them when they are married, and, when they leave, there's no one to look after the parents. So, they get it coming and going. Our traditions make it rather difficult for many families to celebrate the birth of girls. There are lots of illegal clinics where people go to find out what sex their baby is before it is born. If it is a girl, they abort it.

"For some who cannot afford such a clinic, they might take matters into their own hands after the child is born. It's terrible of course, and we are trying hard to stop it. Like the attitudes you see towards your friend, this sort of thing goes very far back in India's history. To understand any person in India today, such as the doctor across the street, you have to imagine all the people standing in front of him—his ancestors— and the centuries of tradition and thousands of years of history. It's not simple at all."

"That doesn't make it right."

"No. It doesn't make it right. But it explains where it comes from. To make it right is going to take a long time."

When the doctor was ready to go home, we woke Radji.

Then she kindly offered us a drive. It was a little tricky explaining where to drop us without telling her about the sub, which I didn't want to do if I didn't have to. I said we were staying on a boat on the river, which was true, mostly, and I convinced her to let us out on the road and not come to the boat, and she accepted that, although I think she was curious. I was glad to get everyone inside the sub safe and sound, including Seaweed, who dropped out of the sky when he saw us come to the river. I fed everyone and we settled down to sleep.

I should have fallen right to sleep, too, because I was so tired. But I couldn't. Something was bugging me. I kept remembering the look on the face of the other doctor when he refused to treat Radji. I thought it was a look of hatred. It was so ugly. Now, I felt that I hated *him*. But I didn't like that feeling. It was so complicated! I just couldn't get over the fact that, had the snake been poisonous, he would have let Radji die. Didn't that go against human nature? I lay on my cot and tried to fall asleep but I couldn't. I needed to get out and walk. And so, while everyone was sleeping, I slipped out of bed, climbed out of the portal, shut the hatch behind me and climbed up the bank.

I walked along the road that followed the river. The moon was out and I saw it reflect off the tops of the trees. I walked, lost in thought, until I realized I was standing in front of the doctor's house. The big iron fence went all around his property except for the side open to the river. I peeked through the fence and saw his fancy car and boat, and behind that, a statue of a woman holding an urn. It looked like a Greek statue. Staring at his house and property in the middle of the night, I felt that what was most important to him was money. I thought of the other doctor, and I knew that what was most important to her was people. They were so different. She had told me to try to think of all the generations of people standing in front of this doctor, but all I could see was money.

I went through some bushes beside his property and found my way to the river. To the right I saw an old barge, tucked in underneath some overhanging trees, just the way the sub was hidden. It looked to me as though the barge hadn't been moved in decades. It was rusted and banged up and looked a hundred years old. So much of the machinery in India was ancient. I liked that. Ziegfried would have liked that too.

I was so restless. Looking to see that no one was around, I climbed onto the old barge. There was a cable rolled around a spindle on the stern, and a crank for winding it manually. Curious, I pulled the cable out to see how far it would reach. It came out surprisingly easy considering everything was so old and rusted. I jumped down and walked backwards pulling the cable with a hook on the end of it. There must have been two hundred feet wound around that spindle. I couldn't believe it. I wondered what they used it for. Now that I was standing at the bottom of the doctor's property, a crazy idea jumped into my head. I thought how much I would love to teach that doctor a lesson by tying the cable to the bumper of his fancy car so that when he tried to leave in the morning, the cable would hold his car back and he'd have to get out and unhook it. He'd wonder who had done that and maybe he would remember us and think about what he had done. I knew it wasn't right and that I shouldn't do it, but I couldn't seem to stop myself. I just couldn't leave without doing *something*. But I did not foresee what would actually happen. I suppose I should have. But I didn't.

The sky was turning blue. Morning was coming. I snuck up behind the car, hooked the cable around the bumper and went back into the bushes. When I reached the road and started to leave, I saw two men and a boy turn down towards the river. They didn't see me. I would have just kept going except they seemed to be heading towards the old barge. That surprised me so I stopped and waited. The next thing I knew, I heard the motor of that old barge cough and spit as it started up. It sounded terrible. A small cloud of blue smoke drifted through the bushes. That engine needed a cleaning badly. Surely they weren't planning to take such an old barge out on the river?

Too curious to leave yet, I snuck back into the bushes and waited to see what they would do. Sure enough, the engine coughed, wheezed, and roared into life, and they steered the barge onto the river. Oh no, I thought, they will get frustrated when the barge won't go and they'll discover the cable attached to the car and will realize that someone was playing a prank on them. Then I felt badly because I never meant to play a prank on those guys, and I wondered if I could reach the car and unhook the cable before it grew taut. No, it was too late. There was nothing I could do about it now.

The barge didn't go upstream, it went down. And it very quickly picked up momentum in the current. The cable went taut and began to drag the doctor's car across his property and into the river, and I suddenly felt sick in my stomach. As the barge went down the river, the cable went sideways across the yard, wrapped itself across the statue, knocked it over and smashed its head before the cable finally snapped. I saw the doctor come running out of his house, screaming. All he could see was his car disappearing into the river. He ran after it, yelling, but the men on the barge couldn't hear him, and he couldn't see anything but a normal looking barge going downstream.

I crept back onto the road and got out of there as fast as I could. I ran all the way back to the sub, where I saw the barge pass with the men on it, who still didn't know anything had happened because the cable had snapped and they were looking downstream the whole time. I climbed inside the sub, shut the hatch and went back to bed.

My heart was racing. The butterflies in my stomach took a long time to settle, but eventually they did. I wondered if the doctor would be able to rescue his car. Maybe. I felt badly. It wasn't what I had planned to happen. I should have minded my own business. I wondered what Ziegfried would have done in my shoes. Well, the doctor wouldn't have refused Ziegfried; he would have been too afraid of him. And Sheba, my mystical and loving friend, who loved everyone and everything? Hmmm. I think she would have won him over with the sweetness of her heart. And if she hadn't, and he had behaved the way he did to us, what would she have done? Would she have pulled his car into the river? No. Not a chance. She would probably have visited him again and brought him flowers and won him over in the end. And he would have felt really badly and tried hard to make it up. Sheba was a messenger of love, or something like that.

Then I wondered what Mahatma Gandhi would have done. He was the first leader of India as an independent country and he was a pacifist. I'm sure he wouldn't have pulled the doctor's car into the river either. Maybe he would have gone on a hunger strike until the doctor gave in and saw Radji. The nice doctor told me that Gandhi had tried to help the Untouchables of India when he was the leader. And he fasted to get his way sometimes. Well, I wasn't Gandhi, or Sheba, or Ziegfried. And I did cause the cable to pull the car into the river and break the statue. And I knew it was wrong and I felt sorry for it. On the other hand, he was obviously rich and could probably just buy another car and another statue. It wasn't as though he had been injured or wounded or anything. And it wasn't as if he was going to die.

Chapter Thirteen

RADJI MOVED HIS KNIGHT and took my pawn. "When do we go to Varanasi?"

He looked up at me with great expectation. I wondered what the centuries of people standing in front of him would have looked like. I imagined a whole bunch of men with really long beards standing in rice fields.

"What?"

"Varanasi. When do we go there?"

My mind raced. Oh, yah, I had promised him I would take him there. But that was when I thought he was dying. Surely he didn't expect me to take him now? "Umm . . . let me think . . ." I took his knight with my bishop. I was surprised he didn't see that coming.

"Will you keep your promise?" He took my bishop with his bishop. The little sneak, he tricked me by distracting me.

"Of course I will keep my promise."

I studied the map. Varanasi was far inland. It was far from any coast. It sat on the Ganges River but if I wanted to sail up the Ganges, which I didn't want to do, we'd have to sail all the way around India first, into the Bay of Bengal and enter Bangladesh. Nope, didn't want to do that. How else could we get there? By bus? By train?

"We can walk," said Radji, as if he had been reading my mind. I was pretty sure he was.

"No way! It's too far. It would take forever."

"No! No. Just six months, maybe. It would be a pilgrimage."

"Radji. I promised to take you to Varanasi but I didn't promise to walk there. We'll probably take the train."

He dropped his head. "They won't let me on the train."

"Yes, they will. I will make sure of it."

I needed to think. On one hand, it seemed like a heck of a lot to do, to go all the way to Varanasi just so that Radji could step into the river. On the other hand, it could be kind of exciting. My guide book said that Varanasi was thousands of years old, one of the oldest cities in the world. It was a holy city where people went to die. The Ganges was believed to be a goddess in the Hindu religion. She was pure and would cleanse you, body and soul—even though my guide book said the river was horribly polluted.

I knew that Radji was kind of tricking me—I had promised to take him there only after he had died, *if* he died—but

I respected him for tricking me, because that's what I would have done in his shoes. In fact, there were a lot of things about Radji that reminded me of myself. I thought we were very much alike.

But there were problems with taking a bus or a train. Where would we hide the sub for so long? And though I could probably take Hollie on a train, what would I do with Seaweed? I knew he would hang around the sub for several days as long as he could see it. But I was uncomfortable leaving him for any longer than a few days. And the sub would have to be really well hidden. I would have to think about it a lot first.

In the meantime, I wanted to visit Old Goa. There were interesting ruins there, including some of the earliest Christian churches in India, from when the Portuguese had come to the subcontinent hundreds of years ago. We didn't have to return to sea to get to Old Goa, but we did have to enter the harbour again, sneak past that destroyer and sail up another river. I figured we could follow a barge downstream and scoot across the harbour at night on the surface with our lights on. That was actually legal *if* we flew the Indian and Canadian flags and let the coastguard inspect us. But we'd get stopped for sure if they saw us, and they'd probably force us to moor the sub for a couple of weeks while they inspected it, and who knows what would happen then? They'd know we were the sub they thought they had sunk, and maybe they'd even arrest us. I'd rather just sneak across the harbour pretending to be a boat.

We waited for twilight then pulled out at periscope depth

behind a noisy barge. Radji took his spot at the periscope. He was feeling much better. So was Hollie, who spent a lot of time licking his paws and rubbing his face with them. Seaweed sat around looking bored. I knew he wanted out but I didn't want to let him out until we had cleared the harbour and were on our way up the river that flowed past Old Goa. I didn't want to leave behind any of my crew in India.

The ride downstream was faster than the ride up. It wasn't as late as I would have liked when we entered the harbour but at least it was dark. A few hundred feet from the river mouth the barge veered to port, so we surfaced, turned on our lights and veered to starboard. We could see the destroyer sitting out in the centre of the harbour, lit up like a giant Christmas tree. I was comforted by the thought that she'd never fire a missile into her own harbour. And since we were riding the surface just like any other vessel, she could only detect us visually, which was unlikely in the dark. The greater danger was of someone else spotting us and reporting us. But with any luck we'd be on the other river before a chase could begin.

Radji was really helpful crossing the harbour. He kept his eyes peeled on the water the whole time and gave me constant reports. He could identify vessels fairly well since he had been living in a harbour for quite a while—how long exactly I didn't know because he wouldn't tell me. "There's a ferry crossing in front of us."

"How far?"

"Far. Maybe five miles?"

"Yes, I see it on radar. Actually, that's just a mile. It's hard to tell sometimes, especially at night. Keep checking the destroyer, okay? If you see any lights moving away from her let me know immediately. That will mean she's putting boats in the water. If she does that, we have to disappear quickly."

"Okay."

The mouth of the river was about ten miles from the mouth of the harbour, which was four miles wide where it opened into the Arabian Sea. I steered to hug the shore as we crept around the point at Dona Paula into the river that would bring us to Old Goa. Luckily, no one challenged us. If anyone spotted us we would never have known anyway.

We went up the river in the middle of night. There were lights on the riverbanks here and there but the water was dark. We tied up beneath an old wooden dock in a small industrial area, just below where the map said Old Goa was. I took a quick peek when I let Seaweed out and tied the sub to the posts. The portal was jutting up only four inches; the hull was completely submerged. It was a decent hiding spot beneath the dock, between old barges and old machinery. It sure didn't look like there would be ruins and churches here, but the book said there were. We had tea and toast and went to bed. I listened to Radji cry out again before I fell asleep. It was the same as before; he was crying out to stop someone.

In the early afternoon we snuck out from underneath the old pier, climbed the bank and went in search of Old Goa. We found it right above the industrial zone after we passed through some trees. It appeared as if in a fairy tale. There were ancient ruins and a gigantic cathedral—the church of St. Francis of Assisi. It was incredible inside and out. So were the ruins. For hours we wandered around in the hot sun, exploring alleyways between fallen stones and vast open courtyards and crumbling walls. But the St. Francis church was really special. It was in great shape. It was the biggest church I had ever seen, and the first one Radji ever entered. No one stepped in our way to stop us, although I put Hollie in the tool bag when we went inside. We lit candles and stared at paintings and stained glass windows and statues. Radji asked me a lot of questions, which I found kind of hard to answer. He was particularly interested in angels, and he couldn't understand why there was only one god. Outside, we bought bottled water, chai and snacks at roadside vendors, sat in the shade and ate them. It was a very relaxed and enjoyable afternoon.

By evening, we were still sitting in the shade of the great church, playing chess, when we were interrupted by a rather strange old lady. She was dressed in white linen, like a saint, and wearing an extremely wide-brimmed hat. Her face was old and wrinkled. Her eyes were blue and shiny. She stopped to watch us play and seemed lost in concentration.

Finally, she spoke. "Well, look here—east meets west."

I looked up at her. "What?"

"Where are you from?" she asked.

"I'm from Newfoundland. Canada."

She nodded with approval. "And where are *you* from?"

Radji raised his head from the game very reluctantly. He looked at her but he couldn't believe that she was actually speaking to him, and so he dropped his head again.

"He's from Kochi," I said.

"Is he? Well, my name is Melissa Honeychurch. I live not too far away from here. You two are an unlikely pair. How did you meet?"

I stared more closely at her. I wondered why she wanted to know. I also wondered how to answer her. "We met in Kochi."

"And you're travelling together?"

"Umm . . . yes."

"And how are you travelling?"

Now she was getting nosy. I wished she would stop asking questions. "By boat," I said. I dropped my head and hoped she would just go away. But she didn't. She kept watching the game.

"He needs a bath," she said suddenly, as if it were her job to go around and tell people when they needed a bath. I looked at her and thought: what a strange person. She looked right back at me. "You do, too," she said.

Chapter Fourteen

MELISSA HONEYCHURCH DIDN'T mind telling people what she thought, whether they liked it or not. She wasn't afraid of anybody. I liked that about her. I didn't like that she was so bossy though. But something she said caught my attention. She said she lived in a lovely old house on a lovely piece of land beside a lovely river. She said she kept an English garden and that she had an ancient wheelbarrow, a Jaguar she kept in a garage and a riverboat she kept in a boathouse, but that the boathouse needed attention and she was too old to do it by herself.

"A Jaguar," Radji asked?

"It's a car, not a cat."

It was the boathouse I was interested in. "Would you consider renting your boathouse to us for a week so that we can go to Varanasi?"

"Rent my boathouse? Why on earth would you ever want to rent my boathouse?" She looked at me suspiciously. "Why don't you just keep your boat outside like everybody else? And you look awfully young to have your own boat. Wherever are your parents?"

"My mother died when I was born. My father lives in Montreal. I live on my boat."

"You do?"

"Yes."

"Well, something doesn't add up here. I don't know what it is. Why don't you just keep your boat outside like everybody else?"

I didn't want to tell her why exactly. "I just don't want anything to happen to it."

She frowned and shook her head. "No. There's more to it than that."

I just stared at her. If she didn't want to rent it that was okay.

"I'll tell you what, young man . . . what is your name?"

"Alfred. And this is Radji."

She smiled at Radji and he smiled back, but it didn't look like a real smile.

"I'll tell you what, Alfred. I'll make you a deal."

"A deal?"

"Yes. I'll let you use my boathouse for as long as you like if you will go to Mumbai and bring my brother back to me."

"Why doesn't he just come by himself?"

"He can't; he's deceased."

I wondered what his disease was but didn't want to ask. "How long has he been sick?"

"Many years. I don't know exactly. It doesn't matter now. I never met him."

"You never met him?"

"No. We had the same father but different mothers. I always meant to go and see him but . . . well, life just flows on, you know, like a river. But now it is time for him to come to me. There is nowhere else for him to go."

"Are you sure he wants to?"

She looked at me strangely. "Well, that's what he said he wanted. He wrote me a letter awhile back, when he first became ill."

"Oh. So . . . how would we pick him up? And why don't you just go yourself?"

"I never go to Mumbai. I once had a very bad experience there. I'll never go back. I have an address where my brother has been kept for three years now. A Mr. Singh is keeping him. You could take the overnight train and be back in a day and a half."

"And if we do that you will let us use your boathouse?"

"For as long as you like."

"How far upriver do you live?"

"Oh . . . thirty-five miles or so. The roads are not too bad."

"Do you know how deep the river is?"

"How deep the river is? Well it's deep enough for a boat, that's for sure. How big is your boat?"

"It's twenty feet long."

"Oh, that's nothing. I'm sure you don't need more than five or six feet for a boat of that size. The river is plenty deep for that."

I wasn't so certain. But I sure would love to leave the sub inside a secure boathouse while we went to Varanasi. "Okay. I agree."

Melissa broke into a smile. I wondered what it would be like helping her brother onto the train. He must have been pretty sick if he couldn't make the trip by himself. Or maybe he was just too old. I sure hoped his disease wasn't contagious.

Melissa said she would tie a red scarf to a post at the bottom of her property. We couldn't miss it. I told her we liked to sail at night and would arrive early in the morning. She stared at me as if I were a creature from another planet. "You are a strange young man," she said, then wished us good sailing and left.

I took Radji's queen with my knight, forced his king into a corner and checkmated him with a pawn. Radji took a deep breath, shook his head with disbelief, like a farmer whose field had been spoiled by rain, then put the pieces inside the folding board. We headed back to the sub. It was twilight when we came over the bank and saw two men fishing on the old wooden dock, directly above the sub. Rats. We were hungry and tired. We wanted to eat and catch some sleep before sailing upriver. But first we had to sit on the bank and watch them catch a couple of small fish and put them into a bucket. It felt like the twilight was going to last forever. They tied up their lines, stood there in the dark and chatted. I felt like going down and telling them to hurry up. Finally they left and we could go down, crawl under the dock and into the sub. We had a plate of beans, bread and sardines. We washed it down with tea and went to bed.

In the middle of the night I woke Radji and told him to get up and take his post at the periscope. I knew he was tired, and I knew that he was only ten, and part of me wanted to let him sleep, but another part of me believed that since he had stowed away on my sub, he had to earn his keep. It was not a free ride. That was the part of me that was the captain. Besides, I figured it was good for him.

I gave him a glass of juice first. Then we took our places, I started the engine and we headed upstream with the portal just a foot above the surface and the hatch wide open. Seaweed rode on top of it. As with the other river, the banks were often bare, sometimes tree-lined, or industrial or strewn with barges. There were very few houses close to the water. Perhaps upstream there would be. All the same, I told Radji to keep a close lookout for people. If we were spotted I wanted to know, although I didn't know what sense anyone would make of a seagull riding upstream on what probably looked like the top of a metal barrel. In the dark they probably wouldn't see anything anyway.

The first twenty-five miles were easy. With the engine running we cut eighteen knots through the water. The river was flowing against us at three knots, so our true speed against the bank was fifteen knots, but with all the twisting and turning it took about two hours to cover twenty-five miles. Then it became trickier because it grew shallower. I had to watch the sonar screen closely and zigzag in places, and that slowed us down quite a bit. The last five miles were particularly difficult, and took us another two hours, so the sun was already coming up when Radji spotted the red scarf. He called out excitedly when he saw it. Looking out through the periscope was Radji's favourite thing to do, next to playing chess.

I came as close to the bank as I dared. To do that, I had to pump air into the tanks and bring the hull above the surface. Now we were exposed. I saw the roof of Melissa's house and I saw the boathouse. It certainly needed work; it was leaning to one side like a rotten pumpkin. But it was big enough, although we would have to surface completely to get inside. I moored the sub to the boathouse and dropped anchor too, just in case the river felt like pulling the sub away and dragging the boathouse along with it. I had learned not to trust rivers.

We inflated the kayak, climbed in—all four of us—and paddled a few feet to the bank. We jumped out, I pulled the kayak up onto the grass and we wandered over to Melissa's house. It was a white, one-storey, mortared house, yellowed with age, with a red, clay-tiled roof and tall windows that opened out like French doors. It looked like a vanilla cake with pink frosting. There was grass growing in the eaves-troughs. There were flowers and weeds growing all around the walls of the house, and they looked like good places for snakes to hide. I wanted to remember to ask her about that. Something moved on the roof. Looking up, I saw monkeys in the trees.

Chapter Fifteen

I SMELLED COFFEE. Melissa was awake. I looked down at Hollie and he looked up at me. "There are snakes here, Hollie. Snakes. Watch out for snakes, okay?"

There was a wooden veranda that wrapped around the house. The branches of trees reached down and touched it as if the trees were trying to make the house part of the forest. The monkeys had the run of the roof. I didn't trust those monkeys. I didn't know why, but there was something about their movement that just struck me as untrustworthy. They were small, brown, skinny monkeys with long tails. They ran around quickly, stopped suddenly and stared to see if we were watching, as if they were hiding something. Hollie sniffed at them from the ground. I didn't think he trusted them either. "Watch out for the monkeys too, Hollie." I knew that he would.

We stepped onto the porch and our feet made hollow drum sounds, almost like music. Melissa came to the door and spoke from the other side of a dark mosquito screen. "Well. You made it up the river all right. Where is your boat?"

"I tied it to your boathouse."

"Yes, well, you will have to remove my boat first before you can put yours inside. You can tie mine up on the riverbank for the while. Do come in. I've just made coffee."

We left our sneakers on the porch and entered the house in bare feet. Melissa's house was beautiful inside. At a glance it looked like a museum to me. There was lots of really old, fancy, carved furniture. There were paintings, tapestries and photographs on the walls— mostly old ones, and some very beautiful ones. There was one photograph in particular, of a young woman standing in a field, staring out at the vastness. The girl reminded me of Melissa in a way, and I wondered if it was her when she was young. She led us into the kitchen where we sat down at the table, and she served us very dark coffee with cream and sugar. Radji was shy about coming inside. He watched me put cream and sugar in my coffee and did everything exactly the way I did it. Melissa put a plate of cookies in front of us and I took one, broke a piece off and gave it to Hollie, so Radji did the same.

"How big is your boat?" I asked.

"Not so big. I suppose it is fifteen feet or so. It is a rowboat.

It is very old but very dependable. My father had it for years and years before me. That is the way things are in India—people keep things for a very long time."

I took a bite of the cookie. It was old too. "When did you move here?"

"What, to this house?"

"No, to India."

She looked at me strangely. "My dear young man, I was born here. I've lived in India all my life, except for a few years in a finishing school in London. *Awful* place!"

"Oh." I gave the rest of my cookie to Hollie. Radji didn't. He was enjoying them more than I was. "May I take a look at your boat?"

"Yes, by all means. Come. I'll show it to you."

We stood up but Radji stayed where he was. He looked at me, waiting for me to tell him what to do. "We'll be right back, Radji. Enjoy the cookies."

"Yes, indeed," said Melissa. "Eat them all. I was about to throw them out anyway."

So, Melissa and I went out to the boathouse, and Radji and Hollie stayed behind at the kitchen table. I still hadn't told her about the sub; I figured I'd just let her see it. That would be easier than trying to explain it. But when she saw it she didn't seem to understand. She just stared at it for a long time before she said anything. I just waited. Finally, she spoke. "That's a submarine."

"Yes."

"You came here in a submarine."

"Yes."

"You travel around the world in a submarine?"

I nodded.

"Well, isn't that something? What is the world coming to? Where did you find such a thing?"

"I helped somebody else make it. He's really good at designing and building things. He's a genius actually."

"Well, I suppose he'd have to be, wouldn't he? Now I understand why you were so peculiar about your boat. It isn't a boat at all, it's a submarine. Well, do you think it will fit inside my boathouse?"

"I think so, once we remove your boat."

"Yes, well let's have a look shall we?"

Melissa opened the boathouse door but there was nothing inside. She stared with disbelief.

"Oh! My Heavens! It has been stolen!"

"Really?" I peeked inside and saw nothing but water. "When was the last time you checked it?"

"The boat? Oh. I don't know. It has been a few years, I guess. Let me see. Oh, I suppose it must be ten years or so, maybe a little more."

I tried hard not to smile. I had a good idea where the boat was. "I think I know where it is."

"You do?"

I nodded and pointed down. Melissa looked. "Down . . . under the water?"

"Yup."

We would have been able to see it if it weren't so dark inside the boathouse.

"But a boat wouldn't just sink all by itself would it?"

"Yes. It would, if it was old enough."

She made a face like a disappointed child. "Oh, phooey! It was such a nice boat too. Do you think there is any way we can rescue it?"

"It's unlikely. If it was rotten enough to sink, it's probably too rotten to refinish. But I can pull it up with my sub and we'll have a look at it."

Melissa stared at the water with her face cradled in her hand. "Everything gets old. Everything. Ahhh, well . . . let's have some more coffee, shall we?"

I followed her back to the house. When we came inside, Radji was no longer sitting at the table. He was squatting on the floor next to Hollie in the threshold of the doorway to another room. He raised his head and looked a little guilty, as he always looked inside a house or a building, especially with people around. Melissa noticed he had moved but didn't say anything. She poured us more coffee, excused herself and went into the other room. When she came back, she was wearing a dark frown. Something was wrong.

"What's wrong?" I asked.

"I'm sorry to say that we have a thief in our midst."

"What? A thief?"

She looked down at Radji. "I'm afraid so. Can you tell me,

please, where my necklace is before this becomes a big problem?"

I looked at Radji and could tell that he had no idea what she was talking about.

"When we left the house just a few minutes ago my precious pearl necklace was sitting on my dresser. Now it is gone."

"Are you certain it was there?"

"Of course I am certain! I have only one pearl necklace. I was cleaning it just this morning."

Melissa never took her eyes off Radji. "I'm very sorry to say that I believe that you took it. Would you give it back to me now, please?"

Radji turned from Melissa to me with a terrible look on his face. I could tell that being accused of stealing was probably about the worst thing that could happen to him. He was ready to burst into tears.

"He didn't take it," I said.

"How do you know he didn't take it? You were with me the whole time. He was alone in the house. Who else could have taken it?"

"I don't know who took it but it wasn't Radji."

"Listen, Alfred, necklaces don't go missing by themselves. Someone had to take it, and he was the only one. He's just a street kid; of course he's a thief. Look at his face!"

The word thief cut through Radji like a knife in his heart. I saw that he was breathing very heavily. I had to get him out of here. "Come on, Radji. Let's go."

"Where are you going?" said Melissa with alarm.

"We're leaving," I said. "We're sure as heck not going to hang around with somebody who is accusing us of being thieves. Come on, Radji."

"I'm not accusing you, just him."

Radji jumped up, wiggled past Melissa and took my hand like a little child. Melissa made a move towards him, and I stepped in her way. "He didn't take it!" I said to her.

We went outside and started across the yard towards the sub. Melissa followed us. Radji was still holding my hand. "Don't worry about it, Radji. She's a dingbat."

"What's a dingbat?" Radji asked between heavy breaths.

"I'll tell you later. Let's go."

"*Wait!*" said Melissa.

We stopped and turned around. I stared at her. In the sun, without her hat, she looked more like the girl in the photograph, except much older and sadder.

"He didn't take it."

"Then where did it go?"

"How should I know?"

"Look. How long have you known him?"

"I don't know. A couple of weeks. What difference does it make? He's not a thief."

I turned around again. I couldn't wait to get away. What a waste of time it had been coming here. I untied the sub's rope from the boathouse and we climbed into the kayak. Melissa followed us right down to the bank. She was getting more upset. "Necklaces don't go missing all by themselves."

I ignored her.

"I cleaned it just this morning."

I paddled to the sub and Radji climbed up. I passed Hollie to him.

"Will you just wait for a second?"

Now she sounded as though she were about to cry. I felt a little bit sorry for her but I was more angry that she was accusing Radji of being a thief.

"Can we just talk about it for a minute?"

"There's nothing to talk about. He didn't take your necklace."

"Then . . . then what could have happened to it?"

"I don't know." I looked up then and saw the monkeys watching us from the trees. I had a sudden thought. "Maybe the monkeys took it."

"No, it couldn't be the monkeys. They've never stolen anything from me. I've lived here all my life."

I climbed onto the sub and pulled up the kayak. "Well, that's where I would look for it if I were you." I reached for the anchor rope.

"Will you then, Alfred?"

"What?"

"Will you check the monkeys?"

I stopped and looked over at her. "Check the monkeys?"

"Would you, please, since that's what you said *you* would do?"

I took a deep breath and sighed. I looked at Radji. "I'll be right back." I took the kayak over, tied up the sub again and went across the yard towards the trees. Melissa followed me. The monkeys saw me coming and kicked up a fuss. When I went to the centre tree where I had seen them hanging out as a group, they started screeching at me, trying to frighten me away. I put my hands on the tree and started climbing up. I was in no mood to be scared off by a bunch of noisy monkeys.

In a gullet in the tree where it branched out in all directions, the monkeys had created a neat little cache. The gullet was a deep round hole, the size of a mixing bowl. It was dirty and stinky, filled with bits of leaves and bark and sticky stuff. But it also contained coins, keys, bottle caps, bracelets, rings, and who knew what else. Sitting on top, like a shiny white caterpillar, was Melissa's pearl necklace.

Chapter Sixteen

MELISSA STARED AT THE necklace in disbelief. "But . . . but they never stole anything from me before. Isn't it a terrible coincidence that . . ."

I held out my other hand with a collection of rings, bracelets, keys and bottle caps. They smelled so badly I couldn't wait to wash my hands. Melissa's mouth dropped open. "My rings! Oh my Heavens! I haven't seen these for . . . for over thirty years!"

She stared at me as if I had performed a magic trick.

"I need to wash my hands."

"Of course. Come into the kitchen, please."

I followed her inside, dropped the junk into a bowl she put

on the counter then started washing my hands. I scrubbed them hard with soap. The monkeys' loot was really stinky.

"Will you apologize to Radji?"

If she didn't, we wouldn't stay. I didn't feel like staying anyway.

"Of course I will. I do know when I have made a mistake, you know."

It wasn't easy to coax Radji out of the sub onto Melissa's property again. She was standing there looking so stern, her feet planted on the ground like a goat not meaning to budge. I could tell it wasn't easy for her to apologize, though she was determined to. But all Radji saw was an angry look on her face.

I took the kayak to the sub and told him she wanted to say she was sorry. He didn't know what to make of that but he trusted me and so he came with me. Then Melissa went after him with her arms open wide and that just made it worse. He jumped behind me. Then, when she was halfway through saying she was sorry for wrongly accusing him, she stopped, as if she had suddenly remembered something deeply sad, and burst into tears. Then she was so anxious to give Radji a hug, as if it were the only thing in the world that would make it all better for everyone. But he wouldn't let her near him, and I told her the hug would just have to wait till another time, and she reluctantly accepted that. Then we took Hollie out of the sub and went back inside the house for another cup of coffee.

Melissa's face was red and wet as she carried the coffee pot over and filled our cups. She put another cookie onto Radji's plate and smiled sweetly at him. I wanted to change the topic and the mood. "So . . . we take the night train to Mumbai?"

Melissa sniffed and nodded. "It gets you into Victoria Station quite early in the morning. Then you will have to take a taxi to Mr. Singh. His business is in a different part of the city, not a good part of the city, I'm afraid. I don't know it, of course, but the taxis are quite dependable, even though they drive like maniacs."

"Do you have a map?"

"Of Mumbai? Oh, no, I don't think so. A map wouldn't help you much anyway. The city is so big you'd be lost. No, you will have to put your faith in the taxis. They're not too expensive of course, although you must haggle. They will charge you two or three times as much if they think you don't know the difference. Whatever they tell you the price is, refuse to pay it. Offer them half. Then they'll come down in price. But you must haggle for a while first. If you don't, they'll think you're stupid."

"What about Radji? Will they let him ride in the taxi?"

"Oh, yes. In Mumbai taxi drivers are not fussy about who they drive around, so long as you pay."

I went out to search for Melissa's boat. She still felt it must have been stolen, but I found it on the bottom, like a dead fish, and it wasn't worth saving. I took off my t-shirt and sneakers and slipped into the water and swam all around the boat, examining it. I could see it once I was under water. It was rotten and waterlogged. Its spine had given way and its sides had spread apart, which made me glad in a way because I could bring the sub into the boathouse now without having to move the boat first. I was anxious to hide the sub. There seemed to be no traffic on the river here, at least not yet, but what if a small airplane flew by and we were spotted?

"Are you sure it can't be saved?" said Melissa.

I didn't think she really believed me. "I'm sorry but it's where it belongs now."

She turned and looked so sad. "Everything dies, I suppose."

It was just an old boat, I thought. "I'd better bring the sub in now."

"Yes, do that. You'd better do that."

I was only moving the sub about twenty feet altogether, but Radji insisted on taking his place at the periscope. And since Radji was climbing up, Hollie wanted on board too. I had the feeling nobody wanted to stay with Melissa.

It was a huge relief tying up the sub and shutting the boathouse doors. Now we were free to go to Mumbai and bring Melissa's brother back, and then I could take Radji on his pilgrimage to Varanasi. We planned to leave for Mumbai the next day. Melissa offered to let us stay in her house overnight and invited us to have supper with her. I thanked her but said we would sleep in the sub. I happily accepted the offer of a home-cooked meal though.

She spent all afternoon preparing it. I offered our help, and she thanked me but refused. With a smile she warned us not to get in her way while she was cooking. So, we sat in the next room and tried to play chess but we couldn't stay awake, or at least I couldn't, and I didn't trust playing with Radji when I was sleepy and he was just pretending to be sleepy. Wonderful smells of fresh herbs and spices drifted into the room all afternoon while we sat with our heads back on the cosy sofa. I drifted in and out of dreams. I was on the water, in the warehouse, back home in Newfoundland. I could hear Ziegfried's voice, Sheba's. I saw my sister in Montreal. I thought how much she would like Radji. I drifted and drifted. The next thing I knew, Melissa was tugging at my finger to wake me. "Wash up," she said. "Supper is ready."

I had to confess I was a little concerned because of the stale cookies she had given us, but Melissa cooked a meal we would never forget. There was rice, potatoes and fish; sauces, vegetables and cheese; chai, lassies and fresh pineapple juice. For dessert she fed us squash pie sweetened with honey and cinnamon. I ate so much my belly swelled like a basketball and still I didn't want to stop eating.

Afterwards, we helped her wash the dishes. But Radji dropped one and broke it. His face twisted into a look of pain and he started to breathe heavily. Melissa just stared at the broken pieces on the floor. I wondered how old her plates were. Then Radji took the little money he had left out of his pocket and tried to hand it to her. Melissa turned and looked at him, his little hand reaching out the money towards her, trembling slightly, and she started to cry again. She opened her arms wide and attempted to hug him once more but he ducked behind me.

"Keep your money, you precious boy. It was just an old plate, just an old thing like me. Keep your money, my darling, you've got your whole life ahead of you."

When we finished cleaning up, we sat in the back room and played chess properly. Radji was improving ever more quickly now. Melissa sat and watched, advising on every move. I could tell that Radji didn't like that but he didn't say anything. He didn't want anyone to tell him what to do when he played. He treated chess as if it were the most important thing in the world. And because he took it so seriously I made sure to play my hardest and give no quarter, as he would remind me to do at the start of every game. The day that Radji would beat me at chess, he would have earned it.

We spent the next day exploring Melissa's property and looking to see if we could help with any repairs that were needed to her house and garage. Radji followed at my side and was fascinated with everything. "Can you fix the things that are broken?" he asked me.

"Yes, I think so."

"How do you know so much about fixing things?"

"I had a really good teacher. But most things you can learn by yourself if you are patient and determined."

"Can anyone learn?"

"Yes. Anyone can learn."

The roof of Melissa's house was covered with red clay tiles.

So was the garage. But several tiles were either broken or missing, and she said it leaked when the monsoons came. There was a pile of extra tiles in the garage. We found them under a thick layer of dust. We also found a snake, which Melissa said was a dangerous snake, but wouldn't bother us if we didn't bother it. We waited patiently until it left, which didn't take long once Hollie started to bark. There was a workshop in the garage too. Melissa said it had been her father's. The tools were ancient and coated with dust. Radji stared with fascination. "What's this one?"

"That's a wrench."

"How does it work?"

"Like this." I picked up a large bolt, fastened it in a vice, fitted a nut to it and tightened it up with the wrench. I passed the wrench to Radji to let him try. He held the wrench as if it were made of glass, and he concentrated with an intensity that reminded me of Ziegfried. Of course Ziegfried was a genius. We couldn't leave the workshop until I had explained and demonstrated every single tool. And now there were two things Radji loved with a passion: chess and tools.

The garage held something else, something old and beautiful—a 1958 Jaguar. It was a green-grey, four-door sedan, with cracked, red leather seats. It was so old and rounded, and sported such old-fashioned knobs and dials it almost looked more like an airplane than a car. It had been Melissa's father's car. Now, it was hers. In Canada it would surely have been a valuable antique. In India it was just an old car.

We climbed into it after supper and Melissa drove us to the train station. I took Hollie in the tool bag but left Seaweed behind. We snuck into the car when he was not looking. I knew he would wait for us till we came back, and I didn't want him getting lost in Mumbai, a city of seventeen million people.

The car drove how I imagined a small airplane would fly—with lots of noise and shaking side-to-side over the bumps. But there was something special about it. I felt special just sitting in it. I could tell that Radji felt it too. It was his very first car ride.

Melissa drove as if we were the only car on the road. At first we *were* the only car on the road. But then we started to meet taxis, buses and rickshaws. I quickly learned that driving in India was very different from driving in Canada. Here, people took chances they would never take back home. They drove extremely close to other cars, so that the slightest mistake could cause an accident. I noticed lots of dents on lots of vehicles. When rickshaws were approaching, Melissa didn't move at all, and they had to squeeze to the shoulders of the road. For taxis she swerved a little, but they had to swerve more. Her car was a lot bigger than the taxis. For the buses she had to swerve a lot, and I often thought we were going to land in the ditch. But we never did.

We arrived in front of the train station in a cloud of dust. Melissa went inside and bought our tickets. Then she double-checked to see that I had Mr. Singh's address, told us she'd be waiting at the same spot tomorrow night, wished us a safe trip and left in another cloud of dust.

Neither Radji nor I had ever been on a train. We wandered over to the platform, found a bench and sat down to wait for the train to arrive. Melissa told us to step onto the train as soon as it arrived, otherwise other people would push us aside and we wouldn't even get the seats she had paid for. I assured her we would.

There was only one other person waiting. I thought that was strange. It was a young man playing a guitar. A pack of dogs had gathered around him and appeared to be listening to him. The man looked friendly and so did the dogs. Radji was curious, as usual, so he got up and drifted over to listen too. He just stood there and watched, and then I saw the young man speak to him. The train started to come. Radji hurried back. He turned and waved to the young man, who waved back.

"What did he say to you?" I asked.

"He said, 'Peace.'"

Chapter Seventeen

THE TRAIN GLIDED DOWN the tracks like a long team of
workhorses with silent hooves and husky lungs. It looked as
if it had been over-burdened with passengers and freight for
so long it had grown old and exhausted. I almost had to tell
myself not to feel sorry for a piece of machinery; it was just a
train. The sides were green and black, but they faded into
one colour. The windows looked less like openings for fresh
air than plates to keep the passengers from falling out.

In the time it took the train to roll to a complete stop, a
small crowd had gathered. There were men in dark suits and
light suits, uniforms, work clothes, travel clothes and robes.
Some were dressed all in white. The women wore brightly

coloured saris. The saris were just long sheets of silk they wound around themselves like caterpillars in cocoons, but they were the most beautiful things to look at, and I couldn't help staring. I had seen sari shops in Ernakulum and stopped in front of the windows to admire the colours, but seeing them on the women was better because they came alive with movement. Walking through a crowd in India I often felt as though I were walking in a parade.

We were swept up in the crowd as it rushed onto the train. Melissa was right—we had to wrestle our way on board, only to find a whole family taking our seats. I very politely explained to the father that they were sitting in our seats and he very firmly told me I was wrong. Then he stared at Radji and frowned, so I frowned back. We wrestled our way through the walls of people until we found a train official and I explained the problem to him. He looked at me, then examined our tickets and headed back to the seats where he quickly removed the whole family. They kicked up a big fuss but the train official spoke louder than anybody else, and they moved and we took our seats opposite each other by the window. The train started to roll just as we sat down. We grinned with excitement. Hollie poked his head out of the tool bag on my lap and sniffed the strange smells of the train.

The train quickly left the outskirts of Old Goa and went up into the hills and we were surrounded by jungle and rock-faces and temples sticking out of the mist. The sun went down and dropped an orange blanket over everything. I couldn't believe how beautiful it was. The train kept picking up speed until it was racing along with a clicking and clacking on the track underneath us. It sounded a bit like a crackling fire.

Radji sat across from me with a nervous smile on his face, but it wasn't long before the chess box in his hands was opened and he was setting up the tiny magnetic pieces. I lifted Hollie out of the tool bag and let him curl up on the seat between the window and me. Radji and I started to play a game. In a couple of minutes we were surrounded by a group of men who were studying our every move. There wasn't room for everyone but I was starting to learn that in India that didn't matter; people would crowd in any way they could and no one took offense. One man wrapped his arm tightly around the neck of another man because that was the only way he could fit onto the corner of the seat without falling. And they sat that way and watched for a long time. Everyone was interested in me because I was from another country. They ignored Radji and he ignored them.

We stopped at a station after a while and picked up more people. I saw them rush at the train even before it stopped. I couldn't imagine where they were going to sit. The train stayed in the station for about ten minutes, and during that time some men came on board with jugs of hot chai for sale, so I bought some. Some beggars climbed onto the train too, old ones and children, and they came straight to me because I was not from India. I gave the first beggar—a boy—a few rupees. He went away quickly and came back with several more beggars, and they climbed over themselves to get to me. But the men sitting beside us shooed them away and told me it was not a good idea to give them money. The train started up again and I saw the chai sellers and beggars drop down onto the platform.

It became so crowded that the man next to me squeezed closer until Hollie had to jump onto my lap. Now there were ten people sitting where there was space for five. And yet Radji sat alone with plenty of room around him. Something about him was simply not acceptable to the other people in the car. How did they even know he was "untouchable"? His skin was a little darker, but not that much. They looked the same to me. He was poor, but so were lots of other people. But he wouldn't look anyone in the eye. And he carried himself with a posture of fear and low self-worth. I figured it was that more than anything else. If you ran from a barking dog it would chase you. If you stood up to it, it would respect you and back down. It surprised me to see human beings act like this. No one spoke to him. They were careful not to touch him. Yet they couldn't take their eyes away from the game we were playing.

The train made a few more stops and then, rather suddenly, we were alone in the car. A train official came in and lifted four sleeping berths away from the wall above ours, so that there were now six berths in the compartment instead of just four seats. We stayed sitting still; we weren't ready to sleep yet. Then a few beggars made their way onto the train and came down the aisle. One was a boy about my age. He didn't have any legs. They were cut off at the trunk, and he wasn't actually standing but holding himself up with his hands. He didn't have crutches. He stood about as high as a large dog. One of his hands was only a ball of skin, like a club, and yet he was swinging himself along the floor and into each compartment like a monkey, to beg. In spite of how shocking that was, it was something else about him that mesmerized me. It was the look in his eyes. He stared at me with such a burning stare I felt almost hypnotized. He looked so intensely angry and yet resigned at the same time. He was my age and yet he looked a thousand years old.

I couldn't move fast enough to get my money out, and, unlike the other beggars, he wouldn't wait. Somehow I think he didn't really want my money. He was just going through the act of begging because that was what was expected of him. After he left, and the train pulled away, Radji said that he was probably a snake victim. That's what happens to you sometimes if you don't die. Oh. I stared out the window at the stars blinking over the black hills and the occasional lights flickering out of the jungle and wondered what had really happened to him, and what would happen to him now. I would never forget the look he gave me. If people could speak with their eyes, then I was sure he was yelling at the top of his lungs. But I couldn't understand his language.

At the next stop, a large group of nursing students climbed on board. They were on vacation and were excited. Although they were older than me, the way they were laughing and giggling made them seem younger. They sounded like a flock of birds. They climbed noisily onto the train in a wave, saw us and crowded in, around and above us. They sat five or six to a berth designed for one. They didn't treat Radji any differently from anyone else, which was refreshing. In fact, they took a shine to him and pressed right up to him until he was squeezed against the window like me. This made it harder for him to concentrate on the game. I took advantage of that and pulled a four-move checkmate on him, and he became flushed and had to take a break. It was time to take a break anyway. Then, the girls began to sing.

They were probably singing in Hindi. It was really beautiful. Radji and I sat and listened with grins on our faces while the girls filled the train with their voices. They passed Hollie from lap to lap and he didn't mind at all. They weren't the least bit shy, probably because there were so many of them together.

After a while, the girls cleared a small space in the doorway and one very pretty girl in the most beautiful sari appeared. While the other girls sang for her, she performed a traditional Indian dance. She told a story with the movements of her body. This was now the most beautiful thing I had seen in India. I didn't even know it was possible to move like this. It was as if she had turned her body into water and wind. She floated and she swam and she soared like a bird. On through the night the train rolled while the girls sang and she danced story after story. It was one of the most magical experiences of my whole life.

The nurses got off at another station to catch a train heading east. The train grew quiet again, except for the clicking and clacking. Radji and I lay down on our berths. Hollie curled up by my feet and we all fell asleep for a few hours. We were not even disturbed by the train entering the vast, over-populated metropolis of Mumbai. The train rolled on until it entered the great old Victoria Terminal, the largest train station ever built by the British Empire.

Like a ball that kept rolling after coming down a hill, slowly losing its speed, as if not wanting to stop at all, the train came in at only a few feet per second, then just inches per second, and then stopped without any jarring whatsoever. You only knew you had stopped by looking out the window and seeing no movement, which seemed strange now. But a lady's sharp voice over the loudspeakers told us we were inside an enormous building—the station—in the very early hours of morning. I reached over and nudged Radji. "It's time to go, Radji. We're here."

Chapter Eighteen

IT WAS THE BUSIEST TRAIN station in all of Asia, according to my guide book. We had a hard time finding our way out of it. I put Hollie in the tool bag but could feel him moving around trying to sniff everything. And there was a lot to sniff. You would have thought we had fallen through time a hundred years, because porters were pushing around old wooden carts, carrying goods wrapped in burlap and white cotton sacks. Men and boys in bare feet were carrying bundles of newspapers and baskets of spices and fish on their heads. Some of the baskets were so heavy the men could barely walk straight. It was early still, and I had the feeling that a very great and very old city was just waking up.

We found the main entrance finally. It was still dark out. There were trucks unloading in the front, old lorries with vegetables, fruit, newspapers and white and brown bundles that the porters were having placed on their heads so that they could race them into the station before collapsing under their weight. Some men were carrying large buckets filled with ice and fish, half the size of their bodies, on their heads. I couldn't imagine how they could possibly carry them but they were, though I noticed their legs looked permanently bowed from a lifetime of such heavy work. They were beasts of burden.

Also outside, many people were waking and washing on the sidewalks in front of the station. Whole families were gathered there. Mothers emptied large plastic bottles of water over their babies and young children, just as we had seen in Kochi. The children cried while their older brothers and sisters laughed.

We went to the front of a row of rickshaw taxis, the three-wheeled, motorized ones, and I handed the address to the first driver. He nodded firmly and said, "Yes, I will take you there. Six hundred rupees." I shook my head and made a face as if he had just said the dumbest thing I ever heard. "It is very far," he said. "Five hundred rupees."

I reached in and took my paper back and looked at the next rickshaw in the line.

"It is a very dangerous neighbourhood," said the driver. "I can take you there safely. Five hundred rupees."

"I'm sorry," I said, "I only want to pay three hundred rupees."

He looked disgusted. "No. Too far."

"It's not so far," I said, as if I knew what I was talking about. I didn't. Eventually we settled on four hundred rupees. Radji, Hollie and I climbed into the back and the rickshaw took off.

It was a dangerous drive and I thought the driver was crazy. He swung back and forth on the street, getting out of the way of trucks and buses only at the very last second. I had to tell myself that this was normal in India and that millions of people travelled like this every day and didn't get killed.

"You are from America?"

"No. Canada."

"Canada?"

"Yes."

"Canada is a good country."

"I think so too."

"Why do you come here?"

"To India? Or to Mumbai?"

"To Mumbai."

"We have to pick up someone and take him on the train." He turned around and looked at Radji. "A boy?"

"No. An old man."

"An old man?"

"Yes."

"The old man must be very poor."

"Why?"

He pointed to the address. "If he lives here, he must be very poor." He turned and looked at me. "You must be careful here. This is a dangerous part of Mumbai. Very dangerous."

"Oh. I didn't know that. Can you wait for us and take us back to the train station?"

He tossed his head back and forth. "Ahhh . . . I don't know. Maybe."

At the moment, I couldn't imagine anything more dangerous than being in the back of his rickshaw. "Why is it so dangerous there?"

"Very poor. Very much crime."

"Oh. I would appreciate it if you could wait for us. We won't be long."

"Maybe I will wait for you."

We travelled for a while on wide streets where there were buses and cars and trucks. There were also men pulling carts and trolleys with everything imaginable on them. Some things were unbelievable, such as one cart carrying the slaughtered carcasses of dozens of cows, or goats, I couldn't tell exactly what they were. I just couldn't understand how a single man, a small man, could pull such a weight, except that the cart must have been balanced perfectly. Still, it was an enormous amount of work, and I could see it in the man's face and his body's posture. And either he was ashamed for pulling dead, stinky carcasses through the city, or I was imagining that he was. It looked like it but I couldn't really know.

Then the driver made a few sharp turns and we left the wide streets for narrower ones. Suddenly people and cows were right outside the windows and we had to slow down. We were inside the inner neighbourhoods of the city now, and they were getting poorer at every turn, and that wasn't my imagination. Then we came around a corner and I saw something upsetting.

There was a monument in the centre where the street split in two. The monument was a sculpture of a skinny old man walking hand in hand with a young boy. I was pretty sure it was Gandhi. On the ground in front of the statue, sitting in the dirt, were four very young kids. In fact, one of them was a baby. They were only partly dressed. They had no pants or underwear. An older boy, about seven or eight years old, was dodging traffic as he was trying to lift the kids out of the dangerous spot in the middle of the street. What were they doing there in the first place? They were filthy. So was the boy who was moving them, one at a time like a mother cat moving her kittens. He looked confused, as if he had nowhere to take them. It looked so desperate, so hopeless, and yet none of the kids were crying. I looked at the driver. I wondered if he saw them. Well, he must have; they were right in front of him. But he just went around them like everyone else, and he didn't even slow down.

I felt anxious for the kids, yet wouldn't know how to help them. There were *so* many people here, so many extremely poor people. Where would you start? I supposed you'd have to move here and live here. And you'd have to have some training on what to do, and some support. You couldn't come here alone. You would be swallowed up in the endless poverty and very quickly overwhelmed.

The streets were such a maze. Now I could understand why it was dangerous. If you got lost, or hurt, how would you ever find your way out? Would anyone help you? There were so many desperate people, maybe you would get robbed and be left stranded. Maybe you would be beaten or killed. I could sort of understand how desperate people might beat rich people out of frustration and anger, and rob them, as terrible as it was. But I could never understand why rich people in fancy neighbourhoods would beat innocent people like Radji. Yet that's what he had been afraid of.

The streets grew narrower and darker. People started paying more attention to our rickshaw, looking in the windows as if wondering what we were doing here. I couldn't help feeling a little nervous but was determined not to be afraid. The driver shook his head. "It is a dangerous neighbourhood."

"Will you wait for us?"

"Maybe."

I was starting to wonder if his "maybe" actually meant "no." And what about Melissa's brother? He must have been very poor indeed. Why else would he be in such a place?

We went ever deeper into this chaos until the driver came to a stop.

"Is it here?"

He pointed down a dark street. "There. You'll have to walk in there. I cannot go in there, I won't get out."

I didn't know if he meant he couldn't fit, or if they wouldn't let him out. "Will you wait here?"

He looked impatient. "Four hundred rupees."

"Okay. Here."

We got out of the rickshaw. I pulled Hollie onto my back. Radji took my hand. People on the street stared suspiciously at us. I tried to ignore them and searched for the numbers on the buildings, which were almost impossible to find underneath the dirt. These must have once been new, clean buildings with shops and workshops in them. Now they were filthy, and many were shut or just filled with people and junk. But some of them still appeared to be functioning as workshops where people were fixing things and maybe selling them. There was nothing new for sale, only old things that were fixed up. In fact, it sort of looked like a community of recyclers, and that was kind of cool. Ziegfried would have enjoyed seeing that, although he wouldn't like the mess.

Suddenly, I had an idea. With Radji in hand I ducked into a makeshift shop where a man was sitting at a workbench straightening copper wire. On the floor, which was just earth, were large piles of copper wire twisted up in impossible messes. Some of it was still attached to pieces of pipe or wood. It must have been pulled out of old buildings. The man was carefully unwinding it and straightening it by running it slowly through two wheels, like rolling wet clothes through an old fashioned ringer washer. A group of four or five other men and boys were hanging around the shop watching. Their eyes opened wide when they saw us enter. I did my very best not to look nervous at all or too interested.

"Good looking copper," I said.

He didn't look up but I knew he saw me. "Copper is copper."

I picked up one clump. "No. This is better copper than that."

He looked up now. "You are right. Do you buy copper?"

"No, but I have a friend who does. He would like this copper very much but he is far away."

"How far?"

"Canada."

I thought for a second that he almost smiled. "That is far."

"Maybe I could buy a little of your copper and bring it to him as a gift. He would like copper that had come all the way from India."

He stared at me to see if I was being serious. "One hundred rupees for that piece," he said.

I did my best to frown. "I can only pay fifty rupees."

This time I was sure he smiled just a tiny bit. "Eighty rupees and you can take it back to Canada."

I should have argued more but was too anxious. I pulled the bills out of my pocket, flipped through them and handed him eighty rupees. I was a little nervous waving money around, but if they were thieves there wasn't much we could do about it anyway. Something told me they weren't thieves.

He took the money and squinted at me. "But that is not why you are here."

"No. That's true. But my friend really would like a present of copper from India. And he will send you a postcard to thank you. That is the sort of man he is."

He considered for a moment. "You have a nice friend."

"He is. He is the one who taught me about copper and many other things."

"But that is not why you are here. Why are you here?"

"I'm looking for an old man."

He looked puzzled. "You look for an old man here? Who could that be?"

"He is staying with Mr. Singh. At this address." I handed him the paper. He took it, read it and looked confused.

"He is dead?"

"No. But I think he is very sick."

"He must be dead."

"Why must he be dead?"

"If he is staying with Mr. Singh, he must be dead. Come. I will take you."

He gestured to a boy in the shop who rushed over and took his spot when he got up. The boy immediately took over the task of straightening the wire as if he had been just waiting to do it. We followed the man down the street until we were standing in front of another shop that was lined inside with urns. The urns were everywhere. There was a very old man there. The coppersmith spoke to him and he came out to greet us. He was very friendly. I was pretty sure he was a Sikh. He wore a long white turban wrapped around his head and had thick white eyebrows. His eyes were unusually large and kind. For some reason he reminded me of a very skinny version of Santa Claus.

"You are looking for someone?" he asked.

"Yes. I am looking for the brother of Melissa Honeychurch. She said that she called you."

I handed him the paper with her brother's name on it. He took it, read it and started nodding his head and never stopped. He went back inside his shop and started fiddling around with the urns. He picked up one and put it down. He picked up another and put it down, then another. He came halfway out with an urn in his hands, then went back inside and put it back down. Finally, he settled on one, a brown and grey one with a silver strip around it. He carried it out and handed it to me. "Here he is."

Chapter Nineteen

AT THE OLD GOA TRAIN station in the middle of the night Melissa reached out her arms and I handed her the urn. If she were terribly upset finding out that her brother was dead she didn't show it. She took the urn as if it were a soccer ball or something, tucked it under her arm and continued talking. "I can't thank you enough for getting him for me. I hope it wasn't too difficult. Mumbai is such an awful city. I just couldn't go there. Funny, isn't it, to meet one's brother only after his life is all over? I don't know a thing about him." She looked at the urn and sighed. "Come. You two must be dead tired. I'll take you home and you can go to bed. Your seagull is just fine. What a strange bird! I've never seen anything like it. He's been chasing away the monkeys!"

I guessed she had known all along.

On what was maybe the brightest Sunday morning I ever saw, we took a pile of clay tiles from the garage and laid the old ladder against the roof of the house. The monkeys were watching from the trees but Seaweed had taken a spot on top of the roof and was behaving aggressively towards them, I didn't know why. He just didn't seem to like them. Seagulls from Newfoundland were bigger than seagulls from anywhere else, and probably tougher.

Radji took to assisting me as if we were performing a religious ceremony. The roof had a low pitch; there was little risk of falling. And the fall wouldn't kill you; still, I warned him to be careful. I carried some tiles up in the tool bag with a hammer and nails. Radji came up behind me and climbed carefully onto the roof. The tiles were dry and dusty and not slippery at all, although they were too hot to sit on for long.

I had never replaced clay tiles before but it looked like a simple task. Each tile had a hole in it for a nail, and each one interlocked with the tiles above and below it. Well, it would have been simple if we could have just hammered the nails through the holes into the roof, but every tile we wanted to replace had an older tile above it and in the way of the nail hole. We could slide the tile in place but couldn't hammer in the nail. After half an hour or so, I was sweating so much my hands were slippery and I was frustrated. It didn't help that

Radji kept sticking his fingers in under the tiles while I was trying to figure it out.

Then he said he had an idea and went down the ladder to get something. "Be careful," I said. He returned with a sharp, hooked tool I had never seen before and a long punch. To my amazement, he slid the hook underneath a tile and cut a pilot hole for the nail in the roof. Then he put the nail in place, but at an awkward angle. That's where the punch came in. By fitting the punch onto the head of the nail, and hitting the punch with the hammer, we could drive the nail into the roof. It was a great idea. But Radji didn't have the strength or the coordination to hold the nail and punch in place and hit it with the hammer at the same time. But I did. It worked perfectly. I was so impressed. "Radji, that's fantastic!" I was so pleased that I stood right up, lost my balance and fell off the roof.

I hit the ground really hard, but it wasn't a long way down. Still, it knocked the wind out of me. I rolled over and looked up at Radji looking down at me. "Are you okay?" he asked.

I got to my feet, brushed the dirt off my clothes, felt my bones and head. Nothing seemed to be broken. "I guess so. It really hurt."

Then Melissa came around the corner with a pitcher of lemonade and two glasses. She was wearing her white, wide-brimmed sun hat. "How is it going, boys?" She poured a glass and handed it to me.

My hand was shaking as I reached for the glass but I tried

to hide it. "Thank you. It's going great. We figured it out."

"Did you? Well, that's just wonderful!" She looked up and threw Radji an affectionate smile, but he looked away.

"I'll bring him up a glass," I said.

"Won't he come down?" said Melissa, looking a little hurt.

"Umm . . . I don't think so. He gets pretty intense when he's concentrating."

"I see. Well. Okay then." She poured another glass and looked out from beneath her sun hat. "It's very nice to have men working around the house again."

"Your roof really needs the attention. We'll finish it up before we leave for Varanasi."

Melissa curled up the front of her hat with one hand so that she could look into my eyes. "Yes, I've been meaning to talk to you about that."

"You have?"

"Yes."

"Why?"

"Well, I thought maybe . . . maybe I could come too."

"To Varanasi?"

"Yes. You see, I have these ashes. And my brother was a Hindu, like his mother's people. So, I suppose the thing I ought to do is put his ashes in the river. In the Ganges. And since you two are planning to go there anyway, why don't we just go together? We can go in my car."

I stared at her. I wondered if I wanted to travel so far with her. It would take at least a few days to get there by car, and a few back. That was a long time to sit together in a car. And I bet Radji wouldn't like it very much. We had been planning to take the train. We liked travelling by train. I took a deep breath and just stared back at her. I really didn't know what to say.

Melissa's face softened. Her shoulders dropped. I wondered for a moment if she was going to cry. Then it occurred to me that maybe she was sad about her brother after all, even though she had never known him. Maybe she wished she had known him. I knew what that felt like. I had never known my mother.

"Sure. Okay."

"Oh, good! Oh, I'm so glad! We'll have a good time. We'll make a real trip of it. It will be a true pilgrimage." She beamed and looked up at Radji, then hugged me. It hurt. I was sore all over.

We finished replacing the tiles on the roof of the house by suppertime. Melissa brought us lemonade six times, and prepared us a feast, which we greatly appreciated. Even Radji smiled at her a little. We washed up and came to the table. Radji explained carefully how we had fitted every tile in place, and how difficult and complicated it was to nail them down. He spoke carefully, with precise detail, like an experienced worker. He had a right to be proud. Melissa listened as if it were the most important thing she had ever heard. After supper we hit the sofa. Radji curled up with Hollie and started to fall asleep immediately.

I wanted to find a map. Melissa had a drawer full of maps that had belonged to her father. Some were a hundred years old! They were great if you wanted to travel to Varanasi by elephant. Then Melissa brought me a topographical map that was fairly new. It had roads on it too. I was impressed. I opened it on the floor, knelt down and studied it. Radji wiped his sleepy eyes, slipped off the sofa, knelt down beside me and studied it too. Though he couldn't read or write, the map fascinated him. That didn't surprise me; everything fascinated Radji.

"What's that?"

"That's a road."

"What's that?"

"That's a river."

"Where is the Ganges?"

"Up here."

"Is that far?"

"Yes."

"What's that?"

"Mountains."

"Ohhhhhh. So many."

"The Himalayas. Biggest mountains in the world."

"Will we see them?"

"No. We go from here . . . to here."

The roads looked like a thousand pieces of string twisted up in knots. What a mess! I took a pencil and very gently followed a route out of Goa. It twisted due north so I abandoned it and tried another one. It went south. Then I found a good one. It was the Number 7. It twisted around a bit but kept going in a northeast direction, finding its way through the mess. It appeared to follow the ridges of a plateau for a while, went past some animal reserves, water reservoirs, woods and jungle. Then it levelled out and ran through a drier, flatter terrain. Maybe it was a desert, I couldn't tell for sure. It wound north with persistence, as if its purpose was to bring us right to Varanasi.

"Did you find one?" Radji asked.

"Yes. I think so."

I showed him and he traced the road with his finger as if it were the route to a secret cave filled with treasure. "Can we walk?"

"No way! It would take forever. We're not walking. We're going to drive in Melissa's car."

I could tell by the look on his face that Radji didn't like that. Too bad about him. He was lucky he was getting to go in the first place.

He was quiet for a little while, thinking it over, no doubt. "How long will it take?"

"Probably two or three days of driving, depends on the roads, how busy they are and everything."

"Roads are always busy."

"It'll be really interesting to drive there. It might even be fun."

"What about the train?"

I looked Radji in the eye. The little rascal. "We're going in the car with Melissa." He could take it or leave it as far as I was concerned.

"She smells funny."

"It's called perfume."

Chapter Twenty

BUT WHAT WAS I GOING to do with Seaweed? He wouldn't be happy sitting in the car so long, that was for sure. I didn't want to leave him behind either; we'd be gone too long. If he didn't see us for that many days he might drift away. I couldn't risk that. But if he were following us through the air, how would we know when he had stopped to rest? And how would he spot us when we were swept up in the traffic of a big city? It wouldn't be like following the sub at sea.

The answer came to me as I passed one of the old photos on the wall. It was a picture of the Jaguar when it was brand new. It was probably her father sitting at the wheel. On the roof was a rack with a bunch of boxes and suitcases. That's what we could do—put a box on the roof that Seaweed could ride in, and jump out whenever he wanted to. And we could put something shiny in it that he would recognize from the sky so that he would always find us. That would work.

Melissa spent a day preparing for the trip. She made a huge pot of rice and spiced it up and cooked vegetables and spiced them up and filled one whole basket with fruit. She filled another basket with bread, biscuits and cookies. All that day her house smelled like a restaurant and bakery. Radji and I replaced the rest of the broken tiles on the garage. We had the method down really well now. We could have gone into business fixing roofs.

Out of curiosity I opened the hood of Melissa's car. Wrapped around the engine I found what looked like a dirty old strap, which turned out to be a dead snake. That made me wonder when she had last changed the oil. Poking around I found the oil filter. It was clogged like a wet towel covered with sand. No oil was getting through. Then, I discovered there was almost no oil in the car anyway. I looked around the garage and found a can of oil but it seemed to have thickened into a kind of tar. I had no idea how Melissa was driving around without oil. I stepped into the kitchen door and asked her how often she drove her car. She wiped the sweat and cookie dough from her brow and smiled. "Oh, not too often. Maybe once or twice a month. Or less."

I asked her where a garage was so I could buy some oil. She said there was one at a crossroads just a mile away. Could

I ride the old bicycle that was in the garage? Of course. So, I climbed onto the bike and Radji climbed onto the back carrier and we rode to the crossroads where we found the garage and a few shops. I left Hollie in the house. I didn't want to risk losing him again. While I bought oil for the car I saw Radji staring intensely at one of those posters for skin-whitening cream in the window of a nearby shop. The contrast between the happy, almost white family in the ad, and the wishful look on Radji's dark little face made me feel a twist in my stomach.

Though I didn't agree with it, I stepped into the shop and bought him a tube. It wasn't expensive and it made him happy. He put it on right away. Then, on the way back I had to keep telling him to hold onto the bicycle because he kept rubbing his skin and almost falling off. When we got back to the house, he made a point of walking by Melissa with his arms sticking out, but she didn't notice. She was too busy. I took a breath and sighed. Back home in Newfoundland people paid money at tanning salons to darken their skin. Some even bought bottles of brown liquid that made them darker. It wouldn't sell well in India.

I drained the old oil from the Jaguar. When I pinched it between my fingers it felt gritty. The last bits came out in clumps. It wouldn't have surprised me to see a dead snake inside the engine too. Pouring new, crystal-yellow oil into the engine was a joy, like giving a glass of fresh water to a man who had just crawled out of a desert.

Next, I checked the tires. They were okay, not great. If it rained we'd have to slow down a lot—there wasn't much traction. Luckily we wouldn't have to worry about ice or snow. I checked the spare. It needed air but we could get some on the road. All of the tires needed filling.

Then I found the roof rack and fastened it to the roof. Radji helped. This part would have been easier by myself but he was determined to help. Then we tied a wooden box to the rack and looked around for something shiny. Radji found a round tin plate about the size of a large pizza. One side was very shiny so we fastened it to the back side of the box. I let Radji do that by himself. I went into the sub to get some things for the trip. When I came back about an hour later, Radji was just finishing up. He had drilled five holes through the plate and box, fastened five nuts, bolts and washers, and filed the edges of the bolts smooth so that Seaweed wouldn't cut himself on something sharp. I was impressed. I called Seaweed, coaxed him down with the promise of dog biscuits, his favourite, and tossed the biscuits into the box. Seaweed hopped onto the car, took a peek into the box, looked at me, then jumped in and gobbled them up. We were almost ready to go.

Melissa said that there was a good tent in the rafters of the garage, and that we should take it down, set it up in the yard and air it out. Well, we found it, Radji and I. It was heavy and full of dust. We slid it sideways (after checking it for snakes) and it fell onto the floor with a bang. We picked it up by its corners, dragged it outside and unfurled it. It smelled strange, like the really old smell of an afternoon party, which was probably what it was. But it was a good size. We also found sleeping mats, and Melissa had washed sheets for them. We were ready to go.

The Jaguar was a bossy-looking car on the road and Melissa was a bossy driver. But that was a good thing in India. The front made a face almost like a real Jaguar and I kind of imagined that it warned other cars to get out of the way or it would eat them up! Melissa had obviously learned to drive in India, had driven there all her life, and drove just like the rickshaw drivers, squeezing into every empty space on the road within an inch, even as we raced past cars going in the opposite direction.

It was crazy, really, and yet it is amazing what you can get used to. I sat in the passenger seat, which was on the left side because it was a British car, and Indian drivers drive on the left. Radji sat in the back with Hollie. They had lots of room to stretch out. Radji took out the chess set immediately and we started to play. He would make a move, pass the board to me; I'd make a move and pass it back. Then he would study it for a long time. Because it was a magnetic board the little pieces never fell off.

For the first couple of hours I kept sticking my head out the window to see Seaweed's head sticking up and his beak pointing into the wind just like the little silver Jaguar on the front of the hood. He appeared to be enjoying himself. But it was hot, hotter than the hottest day I had ever experienced in Newfoundland. I loved it. Heat like this grows on you. It feels like a hot brush on your arm and a warm towel around your head. Your hands are always warm. Your feet are always warm. Your breath is damp. If you stick your tongue out in the sun it gets hot.

But there was no air-conditioning in the Jaguar, that was for sure, and so the windows were all the way down and the air rushed through like an industrial fan with a constant soft roar. And with the air came the smells of the countryside, dry smells mostly, and occasionally the smells of fruit or flowers or the woods.

We were not the only pilgrims on the road. In fact, there were more pilgrims than anybody else, according to Melissa. They came in buses, trucks, Jeeps, cars, and on foot. Mostly they were squeezed together in small buses like sardines in a can. Inside a bus that was built to carry twenty-five people you would see fifty or sixty or more! They were pressed against each other in cramped spaces without air-conditioning. It looked really uncomfortable. Why were there so many pilgrims? Why did they go to so much trouble to visit a few temples? I asked Melissa. She wiped the dust and sweat from her brow and answered without taking her eyes off the road. "This is India. Pilgrimages are part of the Hindu faith. Every day there are millions of pilgrims on the roads. It never stops."

I nodded and stared at a bus ahead of us. The buses on

pilgrimage were all painted bright colours, like pink, purple and yellow. They looked like chewy candy or bubblegum or something like that. It was kind of strange but you got used to it. Some of the trucks were painted like that too, even big dump trucks carrying rock and gravel—they had pink and yellow and purple flowers painted all over them with what looked like house paint. And some vehicles were painted like a kaleidoscope; they glowed with brightly coloured shapes. It was pretty weird. In Canada, vehicles were just vehicles.

I was watching the bus up ahead. My eyes were resting on it rather sleepily as it tossed and pitched on the bumpy road, almost like a dory in a choppy sea. I was thinking it was bouncing a little too much for a bus on a highway, but I was too lazy to think anything more about it. You became used to the crazy driving in India after a while, as if vehicles were about to fall right off the road any second. And then, that bus did.

For a second I thought it was just my imagination, but it wasn't. Cars ahead of us pulled off to the side of the road, and so we did. Melissa asked me, "What happened?"

"A bus just went off the road."

"Are you sure? What bus? I didn't see a bus."

"It was up ahead of us, a really colourful bus, packed with people."

The traffic slowed to a crawl, but some people just refused to stop.

"I'm going to go and take a look," I said. "Radji, stay here with Hollie."

"Can I come?"

"No. You'd better stay here."

"Should I stay?" Melissa asked, confused.

I nodded. "Yes, please."

I climbed out of the car and shut the door. Radji stared out at me kind of desperately. He didn't want to be left alone with Melissa. I didn't know what he was so afraid of; I was coming right back. I started down the hill. There was a cloud of dust in the air where the bus had slid down the bank, hit a rock, turned upside down and slid a little further on its roof. I felt queasy in my stomach. I sure hoped nobody had been killed.

Near the bottom of the hill a crowd of people had gathered. Some had come out of their cars, like me, and some had crawled out of the upside-down bus. People were yelling but no one was screaming hysterically. I was glad for that. There were a couple of men who seemed to be in charge. They were checking everybody over. About two dozen people were sitting on the ground holding their heads or arms or stomachs. One of the leaders was finding people to take injured passengers to a medical clinic. When he saw me he asked me, "Do you have a car?"

"Yes, we have a car."

"Do you have room to take someone to the clinic?"

I thought about it. The Jaguar had such a big back seat I figured we could probably take two people comfortably if we shared the front. "We can take two," I said.

He turned and made a sweeping gesture to two men. I went over and helped one of them to his feet. Another man helped the other and we started slowly up the hill. They were stiff and shaken up but seemed okay otherwise. Probably they were in shock. It's always a good idea to get checked out by a doctor anyway.

We went up the hill very slowly. When Melissa saw us coming she got out of the car and came to meet us. She helped lead the men to the back seat, but when they saw Radji in the car, and Radji was wearing that guilty look, they wouldn't get in. I couldn't believe it. Were they serious? The two men started looking around at the other cars.

"Get in!" Melissa said firmly. "We'll take you to the clinic."

They didn't answer her but looked anxiously for another ride, then moved away from us. I stood and watched them go. It was absolutely incredible. I wondered: would they rather have died than ride in the car with an Untouchable? Maybe.

We climbed back in the car and pulled onto the road again, slowly.

"Is everyone okay?" Radji asked.

I turned around and stared at him. He looked so innocent. "Yup. They're fine. Probably just bruised."

Chapter Twenty-one

THE FURTHER FROM THE coast we travelled, the drier the ground became. We drove through hills at first, with woods everywhere and pretty pink and grey temples. And there were monkeys in the trees. Then we reached a plateau, and the woods became thinner and drier. Some of the hillsides were nothing but rock, and there were strange-looking boulders lying around as if giants had carried them there and dropped them because they had become too heavy to carry any further. India was the most fascinating land to explore, it really was. You could never get bored looking out the window of a car or a train.

Melissa was a tireless driver. I was impressed. She drove with both hands on the wheel and kept her eyes on the road the whole time. When she talked, she didn't look away from the road. She drove in two-hour chunks, exactly, then pulled off the road for a fifteen-minute rest and picnic. We opened the boot of the Jaguar and shared a snack of cookies or bread, with water, lemonade, or iced tea. It was nice. Hollie would whine every time Melissa started to slow down and would jump out and run all over the place. And Seaweed would come too because he was always in a picnic mood.

On the first day, we drove almost as far as Wardha before calling it quits. We drove into a large field where other travellers had already set up tents. Twilight was in the air; you could see it and smell it. Twilight in India smelled like water—the smell it makes when it is evaporating. If you closed your eyes you could almost imagine it smelled like fog, but it wasn't fog.

We chose a spot to pitch the tent, not too close to the other campers, and not too far away. Melissa felt it was safer to stay close to other travellers but I didn't want to be right next to anyone else. We pulled out the tent, set it up, took out our sleeping mats and put them inside. We had thin sheets but not sleeping bags. It was too hot for sleeping bags. The tent had mesh windows to keep mosquitoes out. Melissa warned us not to leave the tent flap open even for a second or the mosquitoes would come in and we'd never get any sleep. It wasn't the mosquitoes I was worried about.

Inside the tent we sat on our mats and Melissa served us cold rice, veggies and fruit. We washed everything down with water. Darkness fell quickly and we could see lights in the other tents and hear sounds of families talking and monkeys chattering and even the howling of dogs in the distance. They sounded like coyotes but they couldn't be, not in India. We were going to pass animal reserves tomorrow and the next day, where there were tigers, leopards, wild boar and elephants. Melissa said that maybe we could see some tigers if we got an early start the day after tomorrow. Sounded good to me. How I wished the road was just a river and I was in my sub, and could moor it wherever I wanted and explore to my heart's content. There were so many things to see here—temples, caves, animals, strange geographical formations, cities . . . yet we were travelling with a purpose. We were on a pilgrimage.

After eating, we washed with wet facecloths, lay down on our mats and let the warm air brush over us. Soon Radji was talking anxiously in his sleep and Melissa was snoring like an elephant. Hollie buried his head beneath my feet and Seaweed bedded down like the Buddha at the door. I didn't want to leave Seaweed outside with dangerous animals in the neighbourhood.

The second day was like the first. The Jaguar roared along the ridges of a land growing drier all the time, yet still treed and populated with people, monkeys and birds. I hadn't seen a single bird of prey yet but they must have been out there somewhere. I was sure Seaweed was watching for them. He seemed to enjoy riding on the roof. It gave him the wind he would normally only have at great heights and he didn't have to work for it. Not that he was lazy; he wasn't.

But it was a sleepy ride—this hot, hazy, dry landscape would surely have been a desert if you took the trees away. I didn't know how Melissa could stay awake and be so alert, but she did. She reminded me of my grandmother and grandfather in that way: they did whatever they had to do, no matter what. Of course Melissa had slept, as had Radji. I hadn't. I had spent all night listening to them cry and snore.

I was drifting in and out of consciousness as we rolled along, lost in my imagination and daydreams, even as Radji and I kept a game of chess on the go, however slowly. And then, from the backseat came two little words and my sleepy world was rudely awakened. They were just two words—joined together into one word—that I never thought I'd ever hear Radji say. I even thought it was a poor attempt at a joke on his part. But it wasn't. He said the words softly but sort of how a bank robber might speak during a robbery. "Checkmate!"

"No way!" I said, even before I looked at the board. There was no way it was checkmate. It couldn't be. I would have seen it coming. I jumped up and turned around. "Let me see."

Radji handed me the board. He was so excited he was breathing heavily, but that was the only sign that he was excited because he was hiding it so well. I stared at the game. I was certainly in checkmate but it didn't make sense. I knew I would have seen it coming. I wasn't *that* sleepy.

"Checkmate," Radji said again in case I hadn't heard him the first time.

I stared at the pieces. Something wasn't right. "Ahhhh . . . there it is! My knight wasn't there; it was here!" I leaned over and showed Radji where my knight was supposed to be. He looked at the board, looked at me, and shook his head. "No."

Oh! The little monkey! "Yes, it was! It must have gotten moved. Maybe you bumped it by accident."

"No."

"Well, maybe it got bumped when the car hit a pothole."

"What's a pothole?"

"A hole in the road."

"No."

I stared at Radji and he stared at me. The thought that maybe he had cheated started to run through my head but I chased it out. I did not want to think that Radji would have cheated. I really didn't believe that he would.

"Checkmate," he said again, and he was breathing harder.

I stared at this ten-year-old boy in the backseat with such mixed feelings. I desperately did not want him to beat me at chess, especially after only a few weeks of playing, and being almost seven years younger than me. That was one part of me speaking inside and it was pretty loud. The other part didn't want to take the win away from him when he had been working so hard for it and loved it so much. I really felt that the fairest thing to do would be to start the game over again. That's what I would have said to someone if I found myself in

Radji's shoes. But I wasn't in his shoes. And . . . it *was* just a game, well, it didn't *feel* like just a game. But it was.

"Okay. You're right. No quarter."

"No quarter," Radji said. And then, to Melissa, as if she hadn't heard the whole thing, he said, "I won."

"*Did* you?" said Melissa, and then she made a big fuss over it. I took a deep breath and stared out the window. Radji set up the board to play another game right away. There's nothing like winning your first game to inspire you. We played four more games before stopping for the second night, and I never showed Radji any quarter whatsoever, kind of hoping that it would prove to him that there must have been a mistake, but his confidence in his win was never shaken. I had to accept it.

There were brightly painted buses in the field where we camped the second night. There was music and singing in the air and the smell of barbeques. Radji, Hollie and I wandered over to take a peek. The pilgrims were sitting on the ground: one group for men and one for women. Fires lit up their faces. The singing was soft and happy. Radji stood and stared for a long time. He had such a wistful look on his face that I couldn't help watching him. He wanted so much to belong to a group or a family.

We ate and went to bed. I was exhausted but Radji's crying out and Melissa's snoring kept me awake again for a long time. Then, when I finally did fall asleep, I fell into the weirdest dream. We were at sea. There had been a great storm and all the fish and creatures of the deep had come to the surface to see what it was like. Sea creatures were swimming, slithering and crawling closer to the sub but Seaweed was chasing them away. Radji was in an open dory on the other side and he was drifting and crying. I wanted to go after him but the sub wouldn't work. Then Hollie jumped into the sea and swam after Radji, and I yelled after him. The next moment, Melissa was tugging at my shoulder and calling in my ear. "We must get going if you want to see the tigers."

Tigers? I raised my head. Oh, yah. We were not at sea; we were in India. Cool.

Chapter Twenty-two

THE TIGER STEPPED OUT of the bushes and walked up behind the Jeep while everyone was looking towards the front. Then someone turned and saw it and let out a raspy cry that sounded like a rooster. There were ten of us crammed into the customized Jeep. Everyone turned around and watched the tiger cross the road. Halfway across, it stopped, turned, and looked at us. It opened its mouth into a gigantic yawn. Then, it shut its mouth, licked its lips and finished crossing the road. Everyone was so stunned it had come so close to us that no one even thought to take a picture. It was really beautiful, surprisingly tall, and so long! Its fur was colourful, almost hypnotic. I tried to imagine a time when tigers had roamed all over India, as wolves had once roamed across Canada. Now, there were almost none, except up north. So many people, crowding out the worlds of other creatures. Why were humans so destructive to other creatures? I looked at Radji. Why were they so unfriendly to their own people?

We also saw trees full of monkeys, a flock of interesting-looking birds, and two wild boars that ran incredibly fast. But it was the tiger that captured our attention. It was such a powerful and mysterious animal. I would never forget the look on its face as it yawned, as if it were saying, "I could run over there and eat you for breakfast but I don't think I will bother right now."

It was a two-hour ride in the Jeep for a thousand rupees, which Melissa had generously paid, then we climbed into the Jaguar and got back on the road.

The dryness and openness of the country continued endlessly, but there were more cars on the road now and more shanties and shacks the further north we drove. People constructed shanties in such a clever way. Against the trunk of a large tree they would lean wood timbers and cover them with sheets of wood or metal or bamboo or even grass to form a roof. The largest trees would support three or even four such dwellings. They were structures that a typhoon would easily rip apart and blow away. But India didn't seem to be the sort of place where typhoons or devastating storms would often strike. No doubt rain would come in the monsoon, very heavy rain too. But we wouldn't see it. We would not be here then.

Seaweed sat on his perch on the roof, Hollie stood on his

hind legs at the window with the air blowing his fur back on his face, Melissa held onto the wheel with both hands and a firm gaze upon the road, and Radji kept his eyes fixed on the chess set as we were swept up in greater numbers of cars, buses, rickshaws and trucks. In this traffic we were still hours from the city. And then, as chance would have it, we came around a turn in the road and saw something that disturbed us. There was a rich-looking man standing beside a rich-looking car, which appeared to have broken down, or perhaps he had run out of gas. In front of him was another car, an old, beaten-up car. Out of that car had come a group of young men, and there was something not right about them. We all felt it right away. You could tell that the rich man was uncomfortable too. They seemed to be taunting or threatening him. We saw all of this in just a few seconds. Were they intending to rob him? The rich man was looking anxiously at the line of cars passing and was hoping desperately that someone would stop. And Melissa did. Very suddenly!

Skidding to a stop, the Jaguar sent a cloud of dust into the air. It startled both the rich man and the suspicious-looking younger men. Melissa was as bold as a tiger. It was something I really liked about her. She opened her door, climbed out and went right towards the group. I told Radji to stay where he was and went after her.

"What is going on here?" she barked. She went right past the young men, who stepped back. She approached the rich man. "Are you having trouble?"

The rich man was very relieved. "Thank you, madam, for

stopping. My car has stopped working; I have no idea what is wrong. I must get into the city right away, I have important business. These young men . . . I don't have a good feeling here. We must be very careful."

Melissa turned and glared at the young men. I stood beside her. There were five of them. If they tried anything bad I would do everything I could to defend her but I was nervous. What if they were carrying weapons? I thought of Radji and Hollie in the car. I needed to protect them too.

"Lock your car," Melissa said to the man. "Take your valuables with you." Then she glared at the men again. She was so tough; I was impressed. I tried to stand a little taller, stick out my chest and look angry. But the young men didn't look afraid, just uncertain. I felt it was only a matter of time before they tried to do something, maybe rob the man or steal his car, I didn't know. They were definitely not here to help.

The rich man took his jacket and briefcase, locked his car and walked with us to the Jaguar. He looked at his car worriedly.

"Come," said Melissa firmly, and he did. She climbed into the front and I took my seat as usual and he opened the back door. Then he saw Radji and stopped. No, I thought, surely he won't make a fuss about that now? He did. He stared at Radji, who dropped his head and hid his hands beneath his thighs. Seeing this, the rich man frowned. He turned and looked back at his car with a terribly worried expression on his face.

"Get in!" barked Melissa. But he wouldn't. The young men

started to edge closer. The rich man stared at Radji again and made an angry face. "I sit in the front," he said. I shook my head, though it was Melissa's car. It was her decision. "Get in!" she barked again.

"I sit in the front!" he insisted.

"You sit in the front in your car," she said angrily. "In my car you will sit in the back. We are leaving. Get in or get out!"

Melissa put the Jaguar in gear. The rich man took one last frantic look at his car and the young men approaching, jumped inside beside Radji and we took off.

He looked at Radji with fear, as if he thought he was going to catch leprosy or something. Radji didn't turn away from him as I thought he would. He surprised me. He raised his head and with determination turned and looked directly at the man. The man turned away and stared out the window. He was offended. Then Radji did something else that surprised me even more. He opened up the chess set on the seat between himself and the rich man and set up the pieces. The man couldn't help peeking to see what the little boy was up to, then stared at the chess set with intense curiosity before turning away again. After a while, Radji said in a slightly sweet, slightly irritating voice, "I can beat you." He was actually talking to the rich man. I couldn't believe it.

The rich man was wearing expensive clothes. Every hair on his head was in place. He wore a shiny, expensive watch and big gold rings on his fingers, which were fat. Even his teeth glistened with gold and silver. On top of that, he was wearing more perfume than Melissa. Radji spoke again, quietly, but with conviction, as if it were a simple truth. "I can beat you."

This was too much for the rich man. He turned and glared at Radji with a furious look. Then he spoke back. "Don't be ridiculous!"

Melissa made a quick turn of her head and blew Radji a kiss. It was her way of saying that his place in the car was secure; the rich man was on shaky ground. Radji pushed the game a little closer to the man and insisted, "I can." Then he moved his pawn. The man saw the move out of the corner of his eye. I couldn't take my eyes away from him. You could almost see his thoughts turning around in his head. I wished I could have heard them. I tried to see the hundreds of men standing in front of him. Were they all merchants? Were they all wearing fine clothes, fancy jewellery and rich perfumes? Did they own large pieces of land and fancy palaces? Did they hunt tigers for sport?

As we drove closer to the heart of the city and were swept up in thicker traffic we had to slow down. The rich man continued to stare intensely at the chess board in front of him. He was debating with himself. I saw him turn and look out the window. We were passing one of the very poor areas. His eyes rested on a group of poor people huddled around a small fire in the centre of a road. Then he turned and stared at Radji, and his eyes fell on the chess board once more. Radji was staring at his own pawn that he had moved, waiting. The rich man sighed, reached over with his heavily ringed fingers and moved his pawn.

It was the strangest chess game I ever witnessed. Radji played as he always played, with an intense concentration that took all of his energy. The rich man played with a look of anger on his face, as if he were doing something he knew he shouldn't but couldn't help himself, like playing a game with the devil or something. The devil had challenged him and he had accepted, only so that he could prove himself a better man and put an end to this madness.

But it wasn't so easy for the rich man. I saw as he tried to pull a fast one on Radji, a quick seven-move check-mate. It didn't work. Radji saw it coming! I was impressed. But then the rich man made a really clever move, and I didn't think Radji saw it. Suddenly I felt my gut twist up inside. Radji moved his hand towards his bishop. I saw what he was planning to do but if he moved his bishop he was going to lose his knight a couple of moves later. I couldn't bear it and so I did something I knew I shouldn't have done. I coughed. I coughed when I didn't have to cough. I couldn't help it. Radji hesitated. Had he heard me and understood? I wasn't sure, but he hesitated. He took more time and scanned the board. He didn't move his bishop. Thank heavens!

The rings on the rich man's fingers were made of the finest gold. I knew that because I had once found a small chest with twenty gold coins on our maiden voyage, and I learned that the best gold was a soft yellow, almost like cheese or honey. There were diamonds on his rings too. I was sure they were worth more than the Jaguar; or maybe even Melissa's house, or maybe even the sub. But they didn't actually do anything except look fat and shiny on his fingers.

The game grew intense. The rich man started to sweat and Radji started to breathe heavily. They both lost pawns. Radji lost his other knight and the rich man lost one of his knights. And then, the rich man was just a move away from capturing Radji's rook. If he took it, the game would swing quickly in his favour. I started to get that twist in my gut again. I watched Radji closely. He could see that his rook was in trouble and he was trying to save it but didn't know how. He reached for his bishop and pulled his hand back. He reached for a pawn and pulled his hand back. He was confused. Then he went for his knight but hesitated. It was the worst move. If he made that move he would lose both his rook and his knight. I couldn't bear it. I raised my hands over my head in a fake yawn and yawned loudly, shaking my head from side to side. Radji pulled his fingers away from his knight. I dropped my head in shame. I had become nothing but a cheat.

Chapter Twenty-three

ORANGE AND BLACK RICKSHAWS, pink and purple buses, black cars, white cars, bicycles, trucks and cows pressed close all around us. We were stuck in traffic. Drivers were honking their horns but no one was going anywhere. Radji and the rich man were so wrapped up in their game they never saw any of it.

I didn't know why I wanted Radji to win so badly but I did. It felt like more than a game to me. The rich man held such an air of importance, as if his time, his money and his person were all more important than Radji, a ten-year-old boy who couldn't even read or write, who just happened to have been born an Untouchable, who had run away from home and been living in a hole in the wall of an ancient warehouse, where I found him. Radji was a good person. I knew it. And he had his whole life ahead of him. He deserved so much more than he had, or that anyone seemed to want him to have. Somehow, if he could just beat the rich man at chess, it felt like that would prove to everyone that they were wrong about him.

But the worst possible thing happened: the rich man took Radji's queen. It happened so quickly I didn't have a chance to warn him. Radji had pulled his queen out to attack the rich man's bishop, but the rich man very cleverly placed his own queen in such a way as to force Radji to choose between losing either a pawn or a bishop, and that distracted him; he didn't see the real danger. He moved his bishop to safety, and the rich man rushed in and took his queen. He made a strange grunting sound as if he were an animal but he was just really excited. Radji was breathing so hard now I was worried about him. And yet he didn't despair, and he never stopped trying. He did his very best to the end. And then, something wonderful happened.

The rich man had been on a roll. With Radji's queen gone, he began attacking his other pieces and it didn't seem possible for Radji to stop him. The end was coming soon. Radji was concentrating very intensely on the position of his king, though I wasn't certain why. And then I saw what he had done: he had positioned his king such as to create a stalemate. The rich man didn't see it coming; he was just so confident he was going to win. But he didn't win. All he managed to do was force a stalemate so that nobody could win. The game ended a tie. I couldn't help it; I burst out: "Woooo Hoooo!" The rich man stared in shock. "No! No! It can't be! No!"

But it was.

The traffic moved a little and stopped again. Men pushing carts leaned close to the car and stared in out of fascination at the rich man sitting opposite the poor boy. The sun was high and it was hot but I thought I could smell water. Hollie's nose was twitching wildly. It must have been the river. I raised my head to see that Seaweed was gone. I looked up and thought maybe I saw him in the sky. But perhaps he was already down at the water somewhere, mingling with other seagulls.

Radji cleared the game and set it up again. He always set the game slowly and methodically, as if it were a ceremony. The rich man was upset. I didn't know why he didn't just get out of the car now. It may not have been the best neighbourhood, but he could find a telephone and call someone if he wanted. But he didn't appear to want to. He couldn't seem to let the game go. And sure enough, as soon as Radji put all the pieces in order, the rich man moved his pawn and they started another game.

The traffic moved a little and we went down the street. While Radji and the rich man lost themselves in their game, Hollie and I stared out the window at the pretty pink buildings. The closer we came to the river, the more colourful the houses became. This city was old, *really* old, like thousands of years old. And it felt like it. Melissa kept her hands on the wheel with the patience of an elephant. She appeared to have something on her mind. I wondered what it was. She was squinting her eyes and it wasn't for the sun. Was she feeling nervous about putting her brother's ashes in the river?

I turned around in my seat to watch the game. Radji was in danger of losing his knight again. I leaned closer and tried to catch his eye. He looked up at me. We stared at each other for just a second and he said, "No quarter." I smiled at him. He wanted no help. He wanted to play the rich man on his own. I respected that. I turned around and looked out the window again with Hollie.

The rich man beat Radji. It took him awhile though. Radji hung on for as long as he could. And though he tried to force a stalemate again, the rich man was ready for it this time. The game ended just as we turned a corner where a crowd of pilgrims were carrying a statue through the street. It had the head of an elephant, the body of a man, four arms and a big fat belly with a snake wrapped around it like a belt. "Ganesh!" Melissa said. "The god of new beginnings. His belly is full of sweets."

We stared as the procession went past. The rich man was beaming. He seemed awfully happy for a middle-aged business man who had just beat a ten-year-old boy at chess. He couldn't help himself. But as Ganesh teetered gently past us in the other direction, such that we were all given a close look, the rich man's gaze fixed upon the god and his eyes went all dreamy. Then he glanced down at his watch and was pulled back into the real world. "Oh! Oh, I must go!" He stuck his head out the window and looked all around. "Where are we? Oh, yes, I know this place!" He pulled his head back inside and looked at us as if he were seeing us for the first time. "Where are you going now?" he said. "Why have you come to Varanasi?"

I didn't know how to answer him exactly so I reached down and lifted the urn off the floor and raised it up so that he could see it. He nodded respectfully. "And Radji," I continued, nodding my head towards Radji, "has come to bathe in the Ganges."

The rich man no longer carried anger on his face. Now that he had beaten Radji, he was suddenly friendly and full of energy. He stared at Radji with curiosity. "You have come to bathe in Mother Ganga?"

Radji nodded his head.

"From where have you come?"

Radji didn't know how to answer, so I did. "From Ernaku-lum."

The rich man raised his eyebrows. "All the way from Ernakulum? Just a boy?" He looked down at his watch. "You know you must go to different ghats, to bathe and to spread your ashes?"

Melissa turned her head slightly. "Oh?"

"Yes, yes! You must! Different ghats for bathing and ashes."

"Okay," I said. "We'll figure it out."

He stared at his watch as if he were trying to make an important decision. He looked at Radji again and then he made it. "Turn here," he said to Melissa firmly. "I will take you to the ghats myself. Turn here!"

Melissa did as she was told and followed his directions. We left the main road and drove through narrow streets lined with tall buildings. Even though it was sunny, the buildings cast dark shadows into the street. There weren't many cars here but it was a challenge for Melissa to navigate through the rickshaws, people and cows. It became so narrow and crowded it felt like we were driving underneath things.

We came to a dead end. "We get out here," said the rich man. He got out of the car. I put Hollie in the tool bag; we rolled up the windows, climbed out and locked the car. I saw the rich man talking to some young men on the street. He handed them money. He was paying them to watch the car for us.

Melissa, Radji, Hollie and I followed the rich man between some buildings and we came out at the crest of a hill. Below us lay the river. The Ganges. My first thought was that it flowed slowly like chocolate milk. It was brown and smooth and wide. There were lots of narrow boats, like dories, and swarms of people bathing in the water or standing on the steps next to it. The steps came all the way up the hill. The saris of women spread below us like colourful flames. Many people were in white, and many had pulled their pant legs up as far as they could go and were stepping into the river that was their goddess. It was such a colourful scene. I even wondered if the river could really be a goddess.

The rich man pointed down the steps to a platform beside

the water. There were a lot of steps. "Down there," he said. Then he pointed downstream. "Over there for ashes." Melissa nodded to show she understood, but didn't say anything. We were all a bit overwhelmed, for different reasons. I looked at Radji. He looked at me. His eyes were as wide as saucers. I wondered what he was thinking. The rich man turned to go. I watched him. He went about ten steps, stopped, turned around and stared at Radji, who hadn't moved an inch. He was fixed in his spot. The rich man breathed deeply, stood as tall as he could and looked down at the little boy. Then he came back. "Come," he said to Radji, "I will show you."

While Melissa, Hollie and I followed, the rich man took Radji's hand and led him down the steps of the ghat. He stood out from most people there because he was wearing a dark suit, and it was so expensive. But that wasn't what made everyone stare as much as the fact that he was walking down hand in hand with a poor young boy. But the rich man didn't care what anyone thought. He had made up his mind.

At the bottom of the steps he took off his shoes, socks, jacket, shirt and tie. He rolled up his pants and showed Radji how to do the same. Radji took off his t-shirt. The rich man held out his hand, Radji took it once more and together they stepped into the river. The rich man reached down, cupped the water with his hands and washed his face. Radji did the same. The rich man lowered his arm into the water and washed it with the other, then reversed them. Radji imitated him exactly. The rich man watched this, and then . . . he started to laugh. It was a small laugh at first, but it grew into a great big belly laugh, which reminded me of the statue of Ganesh, as if Ganesh were there in the river, rolling his big belly in laughter. The rich man lowered his head and scooped water over it. Radji did the same. Then he dropped his hands onto both of Radji's shoulders and said something to him that I couldn't hear. I saw Radji nod his head. Then they stepped out of the river and dressed. The rich man came past us, smiled, bowed his head, and kept going. We watched him climb the steps and disappear. Then Radji came. He had a funny look on his face, what I imagined a bird might look like the very first time it flew.

Chapter Twenty-four

THERE WERE THOUSANDS of people at the river but not a single policeman or guard or attendant of any kind, just crowds of people everywhere, sitting, praying, talking, singing, dancing, laughing, meditating, walking around, bathing, swimming, throwing a ball, holding serious discussions, eating, sleeping, and doing absolutely nothing. It was a place to come to do nothing, and by doing nothing, feel everything. And yet, as I stared at the river and forgot about everything else for a while, I felt a longing grow inside of me to get back to the sub and go back to sea. India was a fascinating place for sure. I loved it, and I loved the experience of being here, but I really belonged at sea, as did Hollie and Seaweed, and we were ready to go back. I didn't know what to do about Radji, though.

We climbed the steps and made our way through the co-lourful crowds to the ghats downriver, where there were make-shift pyres for burning bodies and black, charred spots on the flat stones of the quay. We could see them from above. How strange that this was a place where people carried dead fam-ily members, to set them on fire and burn them into ashes and spread their ashes in the river.

In fact, burning a body wasn't an easy thing to do. It took a *lot* of wood. And I had read that many families simply couldn't afford enough wood to burn the bodies entirely be-fore putting them in the river, and that it was common for corpses to float away in the arms of Mother Ganga, charred and blackened, hardly ashes at all. There were crocodiles in the river too, and porpoises, though it was supposed to be terribly polluted now, which was hardly surprising. Yet to practising Hindus the river would always be a goddess.

Now that we were here, Melissa was uncomfortable. She carried the urn like a baby in her arms. It didn't help that this ghat had a feeling so unlike the other ones that were crowded with people and happy sounds. This place was quiet and al-most deserted. There was something a little eerie about it even, probably because of the black stains on the stones, where bodies had been burned.

We followed Melissa slowly down the steps until she stopped halfway. She had taken off her wide sun hat and was standing bare-headed beneath the sun. Her hair was white and thin. She looked so much older here somehow, with her white skin, white hair and white clothes. She had been born in India and lived here all her life. And yet, I had a sense of her not really belonging here. But she did. This was her home.

She hesitated. She turned around and looked at us with a confused expression. She didn't know what to do. I didn't know what to do either. She turned and stared at the river. Then she looked around again, and I saw that she was crying. I felt so sorry for her, I really did, but I did not know what to do. It seemed that this was her business and so I left her alone.

Radji didn't. He went down the steps and stood beside her. And then, as if he were an old man and she a young girl, he reached up and took her hand. Together they climbed down the steps to the quay. Hollie and I stayed where we were and watched. It didn't take long. They went right to the water's edge, stood and stared at the river. They were talking but I couldn't hear them. They looked upstream and down. They looked up at the sun. Then Melissa opened the urn and shook the ashes into the water. They stood and watched them sink. I couldn't see them. Melissa threw the empty urn into the water too. Then she turned and hugged Radji. They held hands again as they came back up the steps. Melissa's face was tear-stained but she was smiling. So was Radji. Nobody said anything. We climbed the rest of the steps and searched through the alleys until we found the Jaguar, and on top of the Jaguar, like a feathered god from a distant land, my first mate.

Twilight fell by the time we were back on the highway and heading southwest. The traffic leaving the city was nothing like it had been coming in but it was still dark before we found a field with buses and tents. We set ours up in the dark, had a late dinner of rice and veggies, lay down on our mats and went to sleep. I never even heard Radji cry out or Melissa snore. We were all so exhausted.

There were monkeys on Melissa's house when we drove into the yard. Seaweed flew onto the roof immediately, and, with a loud squawking and wild flapping of his wings, chased them off. The monkeys might have hurt him if they hadn't been so afraid of him. But they didn't know the difference. Fear is a mysterious thing.

Radji and I helped Melissa carry the picnicking things into the house and we put the tent away. Then we went down to the boathouse to see that the sub was all right. It was. The sight of it excited me. I was so anxious now to get back to sea, though I didn't know what to do about Radji. In some ways he was like a younger brother to me. But I was from Canada, and was a Canadian citizen. He was from India. He didn't even have a passport. He couldn't read or write. I knew I could teach him though; he was really smart. He'd learn fast. Then maybe he could get citizenship in Canada. But did I want him to join the crew permanently? And did he want to? I didn't even know. I really didn't know what to do. Perhaps Ziegfried would know.

I was long overdue for calling Ziegfried. So I climbed into the sub, with Radji and Hollie, turned on the short-wave radio and got comfortable. It would be morning in Newfoundland. Maybe I could reach him. I tried for an hour but found nothing. I wondered where he might be. And then, suddenly, I heard his voice. He was calling me from another frequency, and he sounded so clear. That was strange. That meant he was at another location. I wondered where he was.

"Ziegfreid! Is that you?"

"Al! I've been trying to reach you for days!"

"Where are you? How come you're so clear? I can hear you like you're in the next room. Where are you?"

"Al. I'm in Mumbai."

"What? You're in Mumbai? Are you kidding me? Are you really? Are you really here?"

My eyes filled up. I was so excited I could just cry.

"Al. I'm coming down to see you. I'll meet you in two days at the train station at Old Goa. Okay?"

"Oh boy, you bet! I can't believe it! I'm so happy!"

"I'm bringing a big surprise, Al. A big one."

"I don't care, the biggest surprise is that you're here. I can't believe it. How . . . how did you decide to come?"

"Will tell you all about it in two days. You'll be there, will you?"

"I sure will."

When we climbed out of the sub and went across the yard I felt as though I could fly. I was so deeply happy. I had two days to wait, two agonizingly long days to wait, but Ziegfried was here in India. It was the most wonderful gift I could ever have asked for.

We spent the next two days cleaning out the garage and reorganizing it. It was good to be busy doing something. But what a dusty job! We pulled everything out into the sunshine and swept the floor clean. We found three snakes: two dead ones that looked like old belts and one live one. The live snake hissed at us and Hollie barked at it until it slithered into the woods. It didn't like us following it but we had to, to make certain it didn't stay close to the house. Melissa came out to look at the garage when we were finally done. She was immensely pleased. She seemed to be giving Radji all the credit, but I didn't mind. They had formed a special bond now, ever since Varanasi. She would ask his opinion on things even though he was only ten, and he would give it after a lot of consideration, as a much older person would do. If I believed in reincarnation, I would have said that Radji used to be a very wise old man who had been born again as a boy. Seaweed would have been a great warrior, and Hollie would have been a happy sailor, well, he was a happy sailor still.

Finally, it was time to go to the train station. I thought it would never come. Melissa was planning to invite Ziegfried to stay at her house. Boy, was she in for a surprise. So was Radji. So was Hollie and Seaweed. I wondered what they would think when they saw Ziegfried in India. Ziegfried was originally from Germany, but had lived in Newfoundland for so long and had adopted its ways so completely that I thought he belonged there every bit as much as my grandfather or anybody else. My grandfather's grandfather had come to Newfoundland a hundred years ago. In Newfoundland a hundred years seemed like a long time but here in India it was nothing. There were only two fishermen standing in front of my grandfather. There were hundreds of field workers standing in front of Radji.

We arrived at the station before the train. Seaweed rode on the roof. I hadn't taken the box off yet. Hollie jumped out but stayed close to me. There were lots of dogs at the station, though they were friendly. Hollie could tell that I was excited, and he was like my shadow. I couldn't stop fidgeting with my hands. Radji wanted to play chess but I couldn't sit still to concentrate. So he asked Melissa, which he didn't like to do because she took so long to make a move and she said everything out loud, which irritated him. Nobody took chess as seriously as Radji.

When I saw the train in the distance I felt my heart jump into my throat. I suddenly realized how much I had missed Ziegfried. It had been almost six months since we left Bonavista Bay. We had been through the Arctic, down and around the Pacific, and over here to India. We had been trapped in the ice, thrown around by gigantic waves, caught in typhoons, and I had been shot in the arm. So much had happened. I felt older now. Travelling has a way of aging you faster than anything. Every time we sailed somewhere we came back different from when we left. But this time we hadn't come back. We had travelled too far. We were on the other side of the world and it would take at least another six months to get back.

Ziegfried always stayed the same. He was like a father to me, and a brother and a friend. He had made more difference in my life than anyone else, and if it hadn't been for him, I wouldn't even be here. I'd be fishing for a living with my grandfather.

I also missed Sheba. But I missed her in a different way. If Ziegfried taught me to be strong and smart and look after myself in the world, Sheba taught me to be more aware and caring of people and animals and things. She taught me to care even about little things, and that you didn't have to be a genius or a billionaire to make the world a better place to be. All of the little things that you did every day added up to a big difference. That was part of her magic, and I always felt in awe of her, the way she looked after her animals or watered her flowers or spoke to ghosts. If there were angels on earth, then Sheba was one.

The train rolled to a silent stop. Now I was the one who was breathing deeply. Hollie kept looking up at me nervously. "It's Ziegfried, Hollie. It's Ziegfried!" Hollie wagged his tail at the sound of Ziegfried's name. I stared down the length of the train. Which door would he come out? I saw other people get off but not him. I waited but didn't see him. Suddenly I felt worried that maybe he hadn't come. And then, all I saw was an arm, but I knew it was him—way down the platform. It was such a big arm. It reached out with a suitcase in hand. Then, he stepped out. As big as I knew him to be, he looked bigger. He towered over the people around him. He put down two suitcases, then two more. Four suitcases? Why so many? Was his surprise in the suitcases? No. It was something else. He reached his arm up into the train and out stepped Sheba.

Chapter Twenty-five

※

ZIEGFRIED WAS A DIFFICULT man to explain. Sheba once called him a "divine enigma." He was as big as a man could be without being called a giant. To the small men scurrying around him, who couldn't help staring at him, he probably did look like a giant. But his height and width, and the sheer thickness of his arms, legs and head, hid a couple of important secrets about him, secrets he revealed only to the very few people who would ever get to know him well—that he was actually a genius, for one, and that he had the softest heart you would ever find in a person anywhere. Ziegfried couldn't hold a kitten up to his face without his eyes watering.

Sheba wasn't as hard to explain but was probably harder

to believe, because of what *she* believed. She claimed to be a witch who had lived many times before, a good witch who had once been burnt at the stake in New England hundreds of years ago, but she didn't hold it against anybody now. She was also extremely tall, though not as tall as Ziegfried, nor as wide. She was lean and reminded me of a giraffe. Her red hair was almost as long as her body and had small curls that looked like the surface of the ocean when it was a little choppy— little waves like seashells. Her eyes were bright shiny green and really sparkled. She said it was because she ate a lot of carrots but I knew it was because she was always excited. She was in love with the world. She loved everything and every-body, even the people she didn't like. Sheba was Ziegfried's queen. He said his life was split in two parts: the first, before he met her; and everything else after. He said it was the dif-ference between darkness and light.

I couldn't believe it. Ziegfried and Sheba were both here, standing down at the other end of the train, hand-in-hand and looking our way. "There they are!" I said, and started walk-ing quickly towards them. Ziegfried saw me and waved. Sheba beamed. Then Hollie saw them and ran ahead of me. Zieg-fried picked him up and got a face-licking, and I saw Ziegfried wipe his eyes with his sleeve. His tears flowed so freely. I felt mine start too; I couldn't help it.

Seaweed came out of the sky, landed on the platform be-side them and started squawking loudly. Sheba greeted Sea-weed then she wrapped her arms around me and squeezed me tight. For all the spices in India, nothing smelled nearly as wonderful as her. When she opened her arms she took my face in her hands and looked deeply into my eyes, as if she were reading my life since we had last seen each other, or checking to make sure it was really me and not a ghost. "You darling boy," she said. "Not an hour has passed I haven't been thinking of you."

Then Ziegfried gave me one of his bear hugs, which was what it would feel like if a horse fell on you—I couldn't breathe until he let go. And he took his time. He looked me over with tears in his eyes. "We'll you haven't gained any weight. Let me see the arm."

I showed him my arm where I had been shot by shrimp fishermen in the Pacific while trying to free dolphins, turtles and sharks from their net. He frowned deeply with his large bushy eyebrows and shook his head back and forth. He stared me in the eye and kept shaking his head. "I don't know, Al. It's too dangerous out there, I think."

"No, it's not. I'm more careful now. That won't happen again. Oh! Here. This is Melissa. And this is Radji."

Poor little Radji. Ziegfried was truly a giant to him, and he was terrified. Ziegfried raised his eyebrows to examine the boy as if he were a treasure, but Radji hid behind me and I felt his fingers clutching the back of my shirt. Melissa shot out her hand and Ziegfried took it graciously with his fingertips. Then Sheba and Melissa kissed, which pleased Melissa a great deal. She was so excited to have company.

"How . . . how is it you both came? And, who's looking after all the animals? And, who's looking after the junkyard?"

"I closed the junkyard for a month," said Ziegfried.

"And you'll never guess who is watching our family," said Sheba. By "family" she meant a house full of dogs, cats, turtles, goats, mice, birds, butterflies and everything else.

"Who?"

Ziegfried twisted his mouth to one side. "Your grandparents."

"No."

"Yes. They were only too happy to give us the chance to get away to see you . . . on our honeymoon." Ziegfried grinned.

"Honeymoon? You got *married*?"

Sheba reached out her hand. Among the many beautiful rings was a new, plain, soft gold ring. She smiled as only she could smile and her eyes sparkled like jewels. "Yes. Married." She tucked her arm inside Ziegfried's. "We are so happy. We would have waited for you, dear Alfred, but you were so far away, and we just couldn't wait any longer. We had a beautiful ceremony on the point, with all our family together. And now we are here with you." She reached over and planted a kiss on my forehead. "But who is this wonderful young man so attached to you?"

Sheba tried to take a better look at Radji, but his face was buried in my back. He was overwhelmed. I could feel him breathing heavily against the back of my shirt.

"This is Radji," I said. "He just needs a little time to get used to you. He likes to play chess. He's really good at it."

"Chess?" said Ziegfried, with his booming voice. "That's wonderful! I didn't know anyone played chess in India."

"Oh yes. They do. And Radji is going to become an expert."

"Really?" said Ziegfried. He bent down closer. "An expert? Really?"

Radji reached up and whispered into my ear. "What is an expert?"

I whispered back: "Someone who is better at something than anyone else."

He liked that answer. He boldly stuck out his hand with his chess set.

"I think I remember this," said Ziegfried. He examined the set carefully. Radji was pleased. I was almost waiting for him to say, I can beat you. But he didn't. He probably thought it though. He'd be in for a surprise.

Melissa invited Ziegfried and Sheba to stay at her house and they happily accepted. We climbed into the Jaguar together and squeezed the luggage into the boot and turned onto the road. The car dragged close to the ground and Melissa drove slowly. Seaweed sat on the roof. I heard him stepping around up there. Ziegfried and Sheba sat arm in arm in the backseat. Radji squeezed into the front with me. It was strange to think that Ziegfried and Sheba were married now but it made perfect sense. He had been hopelessly in love with her ever since he first set eyes upon her and could barely speak. Seeing them married now made me think that good things happen to people even if they have to wait a long time. Sheba and Ziegfried both waited a very long time to find each other, but they did. I couldn't stop watching them now and smiling. They looked like the happiest people in the whole world.

Melissa was happy to have so much company in her home. She served a pot of tea with cookies, then immediately set about creating a meal. Sheba joined her in the kitchen and the sound of their conversation took on the tone of women's talk, which was almost like a different language to me. I wasn't used to seeing women together much.

Ziegfried wanted to examine the sub. But first he accepted the challenge of a game of chess with Radji. I was about to warn Radji but then I thought, why bother? He'll see for himself soon enough. In fact, I was curious to see how hard Ziegfried would play with him. Would he take it easy on him because he was only ten years old and a beginner? Would he give him quarter, at least a little, or beat him ruthlessly?

He beat him ruthlessly. He never gave him the slightest hint of quarter. They played five games and Radji never lasted more than seven moves. The whole thing didn't take longer than twenty-five minutes. I watched Radji's eyes grow wider at every move. Ziegfried played as he did anything else— with complete attention. At each checkmate it was as if he had reached out with an iron hand and crushed Radji's king. Radji never had a chance. I knew that feeling well.

Was Radji going to be upset? I was worried he might be. I watched him when Ziegfried stood up to go out to the sub.

Radji stared with awe. Then he turned to me and whispered with a little smile: "He's an expert."

"Yes," I said. "He is."

Radji followed us out to the boathouse. Ziegfried stood and stared at the little river. "How on earth did you get the sub up the river, Al? Did you pull it up with elephants?"

"We came at night, on the surface."

He bent down and scanned the river closely. "It can't be ten feet!"

"It's about that."

He shook his head. "Okay, I've got to see the sub, Al. You said you were depth-charged. Lord Almighty! You never saw a leak? Not even a drop?"

I was nervous to show Ziegfried the sub now. He was so obsessed with safety. I knew it was important but he always went overboard with it. If he felt the sub wasn't safe enough to sail, he could ground me right here and now. It was an agreement we had right from the beginning. I was the captain of the sub, but he was the one who decided whether or not it was fit for sea. If he said it wasn't, it wasn't going anywhere.

"Let me see it, Al."

Chapter Twenty-six

I UNLOCKED THE BOATHOUSE door and opened it up. Ziegfried bent his head and entered. I followed him in, and Radji and Hollie followed me. Seaweed flew up to the roof. Ziegfried rested his hands on his hips and stared. "There she is."

"Yup."

"She's still afloat."

"Yup."

"How long has she been sitting here?"

"Umm . . . about a week, I guess."

"And how long since you put the run on the Indian navy?"

"Uhh . . . about a month, I guess."

"A month?"

"Yes."

"And what's the deepest you've gone since then?"

"Umm . . . three hundred and twenty feet or so."

"Well, that's good. Can't be any leak. Let's have a look inside."

Ziegfried barely fit inside the sub. He had a really hard time getting in, and then he had to bend over like an old witch. He climbed in and went straight into the stern to see the engine. "Start her up, Al."

I started the engine.

"Good. Rev her up!"

I cranked up the power.

"Higher!"

I turned it all the way up. The engine roared. I loved the sound of it. I was suddenly anxious to get to sea. I wasn't anxious to leave Ziegfried and Sheba though. "Should I turn it down?"

"No! Keep her there!"

If I were to put the sub in gear right now, in reverse, it would pull this little boathouse right off the bank and we'd run into the other side.

"Okay. Let her down now. Turn the batteries on full!"

I did as I was told. Radji stood beside me and waited for Ziegfried to give him orders too, but he never did.

We stayed a couple of hours inside the sub. Ziegfried spent most of that time either on his knees or sitting down while he examined everything. I was nervous the whole time. Radji sat with Hollie by his blanket in the bow and patted his fur. I was thinking how nice it would be to have Radji on the sub with us. He was good company and had already proved himself a valuable mate. But I knew it wasn't a good idea for a number of reasons, not least of all that I couldn't guarantee his safety, and he was too young to be taking the sorts of risks I was taking. I didn't know what I was going to do with him.

"Okay, Al. I'm done for now."

"And?"

"Well . . . that depends."

"Depends? What do you mean? What does it depend on?"

"Where are you planning to go next?"

"Africa."

"That's what I thought. The east coast, right?"

"Yah. Why?"

"I am sorry, Al. I'm going to have to ground the sub."

I froze. "Gggg . . . gggg . . . ground it? Www . . . what do you mean? Why? Why do you have to ground it? It's working perfectly, honest!"

"Al." Ziegfried sighed deeply. "Look." He reached over and took my arm and turned it over. "Look, Al. This is a gunshot wound."

I dropped my eyes. "I know."

"And you know that whoever shot you was trying to kill you, right?"

"Yes."

"And how's your hearing?"

"It's getting better all the time. It's almost back to normal."

"But you got depth-charged by the Indian navy, Al."

"I know."

"You were maybe one or two charges away from a watery grave. And Hollie too."

I nodded. I was really worried now.

"And you know what's on the east coast of Africa, right?"

I knew he meant Somalia, and all the pirates there. I nodded.

He shook his head and frowned. "I'm sorry, Al. I really am. But she's grounded."

I felt like bursting out crying but reminded myself that I was sixteen. I was too old to cry over disappointment. Besides, I didn't want Radji to see me. But Ziegfried couldn't ground the sub, he just couldn't. There was so much more I needed to see, so many places I needed to go. Besides, I wasn't just exploring any more, I was learning about the health of the sea and preparing for a career as an environmentalist. The sea was in trouble and needed people to help clean it up and make it safer for all of its creatures. It needed us to protect them. Maybe I would have to go to school for that, and maybe not, I didn't know exactly, but for now I needed to learn as much about it as I could by myself. He couldn't ground the sub when I was only getting started, he just couldn't. I felt panic. I was starting to breathe hard, just like Radji.

"Unless . . ."

"Unless? Unless what?"

He took a deep breath and stared intensely into my eyes.

"Unless you make me a solemn promise that you won't sail within five hundred miles of Somalia from any direction."

I quickly tried to see the east coast of Africa in my mind. I knew that Kenya was next to Somalia, and there was Mozambique and Tanzania and South Africa, but I was so distracted with worry that I couldn't remember exactly which country was next to Kenya except that it wasn't South Africa. That was on the bottom. If I made the promise I would almost certainly never get to see Kenya but I wasn't sure about the other countries. I didn't have much choice. "I promise."

"You solemnly promise?"

He stared at me with a look that would have frightened any man in the world out of his boots.

"I solemnly promise."

"Will you also promise to stop taking dangerous risks?"

"I don't try to."

"Do you promise?"

"Yes. I promise."

"We built the sub for exploration, Al. It won't hold up to what you're doing with it. It's not made for that. We want to see you make it home in one piece."

"I know."

He smiled and dropped his hand on my shoulder. "Okay, then. Let's go in and talk to the girls." He meant Sheba and Melissa.

"Okay." I let out a deep breath. Whew! Radji, Hollie and I followed Ziegfried up the ladder and out of the sub. What a tough inspection.

We sat at Melissa's table and shared a meal filled with lots of excited talk. Melissa was so happy she was beaming red. With tears in her eyes she shared something personal with us. "When I poured my brother's ashes into the river four days ago, I said a prayer. I was losing the last member of my family and I was feeling so alone, so terribly alone, and so I said a prayer. I asked if somehow I could be part of another family. I knew it was a lot to ask, especially at my age. But they say that's what prayers are for, asking for things that seem out of reach. And so I did. And here now, just four days later, we are all together. And I really feel that you are my new family." She wiped her eyes with her handkerchief. Sheba leaned over and hugged her and kissed her on the cheek. "We are your family indeed, my love."

Radji sat next to Ziegfried and fidgeted with his chess set. The difference in their sizes made me smile. Radji ate slowly and listened to the conversation with great interest, answering questions when he was asked. But he only asked one question all evening. It didn't surprise me. It probably took him awhile to get up the nerve to ask.

He looked up at Ziegfried and said, "How do you become an expert?" Ziegfried looked down at him the way he would have looked at a mechanic who had asked him how to replace the valves on a twelve-stroke engine. "Well, you have to play thousands of games, of course. That's the first thing. But it is also a very good idea to pick up a few good books on strategy and study them. Read them over and over. Maybe we can find a shop tomorrow somewhere and buy you some."

Radji nodded but I saw the light dim in his eyes. I would have to tell the others later that he couldn't read or write. But he could learn.

At the end of the meal, Ziegfried and Sheba said that they had presents. Ziegfried handed me a small box. When I opened it I found his watch inside, his beautiful, golden round watch that had been his grandfather's. I always loved it. I couldn't believe he was giving it to me. "No," I said. "I can't take it." "Yes," he said. "I want you to have it. My grandfather would have approved of you having it. Trust me, Al." My eyes clouded as I stared at the watch. It had large black numbers and little crystals inside it. It was attached to a gold chain. I felt so honoured that he would give it to me. "I love it." Radji stared at the watch with wonder, as I had done when I first saw it.

Then Ziegfried gave a small present to Radji. It was wrapped in paper. Radji's eyes opened wide. I knew it had probably been intended for me, but that's how caring Ziegfried was— he wouldn't neglect someone, and he knew I would understand. Radji opened the paper and discovered a lovely golden pen. Radji's eyes were all over it, then he looked at me to see if it was okay to accept it. I smiled at him.

Sheba gave us each a wrapped present. Radji received a brand new journal with a beautiful cover and the nicest paper inside. It was for writing. When I opened my present I discovered a book with a picture of a riverboat on it. It looked like Africa. The story was by Joseph Conrad, and was called *Heart of Darkness.* "Read it on your next journey," Sheba said, and winked at me.

"Thank you both so much," I said. "It's really me who should be giving you presents because you just got married."

"Oh, you have," Sheba said.

"How?"

She looked towards Radji, who was completely absorbed with his book and pen. "You have taken another soul under your wing. Nothing could possibly be a more wonderful gift to me, Alfred."

Then Sheba took the necklace from around her own neck and placed it on Melissa's neck and kissed her.

"Oh, my darling girl," said Melissa, "You have a golden heart."

She sure did.

We started to stock the sub the next day for the trip to Africa. It was roughly a three-thousand-mile sail southwest. There were islands along the way, such as the Maldives and the Seychelles. I was particularly interested in visiting Madagascar, one of those places in the world famous for all its unusual creatures. As much as I missed home, and as much as I hated to leave Ziegfried and Sheba right now, the lure of visiting Madagascar and Africa was too great for me to resist. I was an explorer after all.

Ziegfried, Radji, Hollie and I took the Jaguar and drove in to Panjim to buy fresh food and supplies while Melissa and Sheba spent the day baking and talking. I knew how lucky I was to have so much support from such loving people and I hoped I would find a way to pay them back someday.

We found a shop that sold chess sets and books about

chess. Ziegfried bought a new set for Radji and a couple of books. Radji examined every set in the store, then concluded that the one that Ziegfried bought was the smartest choice. I was starting to notice similarities in the way that Radji and Ziegfried thought, and it crossed my mind that Radji could learn so much from him. I even wondered if it were a possibility, too, that Radji return to Newfoundland with Ziegfried and Sheba, and live with them there, but, as it turned out, that was not what was in the cards.

When we returned to Melissa's, and Ziegfried and I began to load up the sub, Melissa and Sheba came outside. I could tell by the look on their faces that they had been discussing something and had reached a decision. When Sheba reached a decision, going against it was like going against the tide. If Ziegfried depended on the logic of science and mathematics, Sheba used the logic of the universe. Melissa came to Radji and asked him to take a walk with her. Radji looked at me with that worried look on his face; I could tell that somehow he knew what Melissa was going to ask him. And yet he went with her. They walked away from the house and slowly towards the road. I stood with a bunch of bananas in my arms and watched them go. Melissa was doing the talking and Radji was listening. I wished I could hear, though I knew it was none of my business.

I saw them come back half an hour later. This time, Radji was doing the talking and Melissa was listening. Then Melissa hugged him and went into the house. Radji came over to me and he was wearing a smile. "This is my home now," he said proudly. He pointed to the house and the garage and the river. "This is where I live now. I am going to learn how to read and write, and I am going to study and go to school. I will fix things when they are broken and will keep the yard clean and will become an expert at chess. I will learn other things too."

He handed me back the little magnetic chess set. "You should keep this on your submarine, Alfred."

I looked Radji in the eye and put my hand down on his shoulder just as Ziegfried had done to me. "I am so happy for you, Radji. Do you think you will be happy here?"

"Yes. Yes, I will be happy here. And I will work hard, like you, and like Ziegfried."

And I knew that he would.

Epilogue

✕

THE DESTROYER LOOMED ahead like a giant troll on a bridge. She scared me. She pointed in our direction and her bow was sharp and her missiles glistening. The barge in front of me was slapping clumsily through the water like a pond turtle. We were so close behind I could see hairline cracks in her rusty stern. When she turned to port and aimed for the barge terminal I tucked in on the port side of her. And when she reached the terminal I went under her and waited there until dark. When I knew that darkness had fallen, I pedalled out of the harbour as quietly as a bat. I slipped underneath the first ship I saw, after checking that it wasn't a navy ship, and followed it for a few miles out before surfacing. I cranked up the engine full blast, opened the hatch and climbed the portal with Hollie and Seaweed. Beneath a shining crescent moon and two beautiful stars, we headed southwest towards Africa.

Ziegfried and Sheba were on their way to Delhi and Agra. It was their honeymoon, an exciting new beginning for them. That made me happy. Radji was studying the alphabet with Melissa, a new beginning for each of them. I knew that Radji would grow up to become someone important in India, someone who would bring changes to his country, maybe even like Gandhi. In some ways he and Melissa were an unlikely pair. And yet, there was a certain logic to their arrangement.

Melissa would look after Radji to the best of her ability. She would teach him to read and write and give him the chance to go to school. She would feed him well and he would grow healthy and strong. This I knew. And Radji would become like a son to her and give her the sense of family that she longed for so much. And she would be happy. He was young, and she was old, but he already had so much maturity and integrity. When he was older I knew that he would return to his own family and make things right. He was a wise old man in a young boy's body, he really was.

As we ploughed through the darkness of the Indian Ocean and I contemplated these things, I felt that all was right with the world. And yet I left India with a small sadness. I would miss it. I had fallen in love with it. That seemed strange to me in a way. There were certain things about it I didn't like—how some people treated other people. But that didn't stop

me from loving it. And perhaps it was changing. I kept thinking of the rich man in Varanasi: the sight of him standing in
the Ganges, smiling, laughing, holding hands with Radji. It
was such a wonderful memory now. I remembered the nurses
and the girl performing a traditional dance on the train. I remembered the smell of the ground, the heat, the fresh spices
of India. I felt a little ache inside because I would miss all of
this.

Funny, so many millions of people here believed in reincarnation, just as Sheba believed in reincarnation. And so if it
were true, then maybe I had lived here before too. Perhaps I
had even known Radji in another life. I wondered. But I
guessed I didn't really believe in that. Not yet. But I did believe one thing: that I would come back. And when I did, a
part of me would be here already, waiting.

ABOUT THE AUTHOR

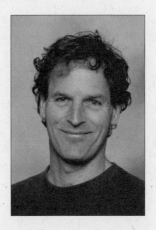

Philip Roy continues to live in Nova Scotia, the province of his birth, but keeps on the road so often he sometimes cannot remember where he is waking up in the morning. Besides the Submarine Outlaw series, Philip is publishing an historical novel this year—*Blood Brothers in Louisbourg*—and has several other projects on the go, including his picture book series, *Happy the Pocket Mouse* (unpublished), already a favourite read-aloud series on his school visits. Philip has just returned from a trip to Africa where he was researching Alfred's next adventure—*Seas of South Africa*.

RECYCLED
Paper made from
recycled material
FSC® C103567

Marquis Book Printing Inc.

Québec, Canada

2012

Printed on Silva Enviro 100% post-consumer EcoLogo certified paper,
processed chlorine free and manufactured using biogas energy.